BOOTS & LACE

UGLY STICK SALOON SERIES #7

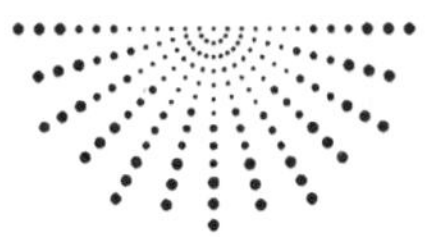

MYLA JACKSON

TWISTED PAGE INC

BOOTS & LACE

UGLY STICK SALOON SERIES #7

New York Times & USA Today
Bestselling Author

ELLE JAMES

writing as

MYLA JACKSON

EBOOK ISBN: 978-1-62695-098-6

PRINT ISBN: 978-1-62695-099-3

*This book is dedicated to Ed and Kendall from SEX ED,
without whom Lacey would never have been brought to life!*

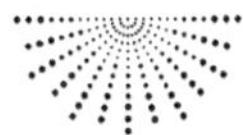

The cowboy at the bar had captured Lacey Lambert's attention from the beginning, with his dark good looks and an expression so somber it made her sad. He sat by himself, head down, staring into his mug of beer.

As Lacey waited tables in the busy Ugly Stick Saloon, her gaze wandered back to him more and more.

Fellow waitress Kendall Mason passed her carrying a tray full of whiskey shooters and beer. "Did you see him?" she whispered.

Lacey, on her way back to the bar with an empty tray, played dumb and asked, "See who?"

Kendall stopped long enough to throw a frown. "Seriously? The smokin' hot cowboy at the bar. You can't miss him."

Lacey Lambert hadn't missed him. In fact she could barely concentrate on her duties with the man sitting in the seat next to where she stopped to place her orders with Libby, the bartender. Every time she pulled up to the bar, her heartbeat fluttered and she forgot how to breathe.

All bad news as far as she was concerned. Flirting, having sex, playing around were all fine in her books, but getting involved? No way.

Lacey shrugged. "So, he's cute."

"Honey, he's not cute, he's…" Kendall fanned her face. "Va-va-va-voom!"

"Now, what would Ed think if he heard you talking like that?"

"He'd know I was only looking out for my best friend. He has nothing to worry about. I'm totally in love with my hunka-hunka-burnin' love."

Lacey shrugged. "So, the cowboy is easy on the eyes. He's probably full of himself." Her ex had been one of those. Easy to look at and easy with the women. Thus the "ex" part to the equation. "I'm not interested."

"Such a shame. I bet he's nice and nicer in bed."

"Not many good-looking guys are nice. And most aren't that great in bed."

Kendall glared at Lacey. "Ed is. And Jackson and Luke and Mark from what Audrey and Libby say—"

Lacey raised her empty hand. "Okay, okay, you've made your point. I don't have time to flirt. I have an order to fill."

"I'll take your tables if you want to work on getting his number."

A cowboy at one of the tables hollered, "Kendall! We gonna get those shooters sometime today?"

"Coming," Kendall called out. To Lacey she said, "Think about it. You could use a man in your life."

"They're only good for one thing."

"Sex?"

"Okay, two." Lacey grinned. "Sex and taking out the trash."

"You're hopeless. What happened to the carefree, happy-go-lucky roommate I knew?"

"You moved out with a gorgeous cowboy." Lacey sighed. "I'm going to miss you."

"Same here."

The customer yelled again. "Kendall!"

"Keep your pants on. I'm coming." Kendall scooted away from Lacey.

Lacey sucked in her breath and proceeded to the bar.

A beautiful woman had planted herself in the seat beside the brooding cowboy. Her plain companion sat on the other side of her. In less than a minute, a man sashayed up to the prettier girl and asked her to dance.

She bounced out of her seat and led the way to the dance floor, the cowboy following.

Lacey's dark cowboy glanced up briefly from his beer, his gaze going to the pretty girl's not-as-pretty friend.

The woman sat facing the dancing, and heaved a sigh, a smile plastered to her face, her toe tapping to the beat of the music.

Lacey placed her order with Libby and made another pass through the saloon, delivering full glasses and collecting empties. When she returned to the bar, the pretty girl was just sitting down when another cowboy asked her to dance.

Off she went again, leaving her friend at the bar.

Lacey's heart went out to the girl. She wasn't exactly pretty, but she had a nice smile and just a few extra pounds.

All the while Lacey took and delivered orders, she watched the bar, the cowboy and the women beside him.

After the fourth time the skinny woman left her chunkier friend alone to dance with another cowboy, the dark-haired cowboy pushed back from the bar and stood, a frown creasing his forehead, the first change to his expression since Lacey had started watching the man.

He half-bowed, saying something to the sunny-faced big girl.

Her eyes lit up and she hopped off her barstool, lighter on her feet than Lacey would have thought.

The cowboy held out his arm, she took it, her smile widening as he led her to the dance floor. They took off in a lively two-step.

Lacey's heart lightened for the girl, and then she frowned.

Damn. Kendall had been right. The brooding cowboy *was* nice. While all the other cowboys had passed the girl by, the dark-eyed one asked her to dance, giving her the thrill of her life.

When the song ended, the cowboy returned her to her seat and bowed over her hand, thanked her and pressed a kiss to her knuckles.

The woman's face flushed a pretty pink and she batted her eyes.

Double damn. Lacey had wanted to count him off as another pretty boy, all looks, no substance, and he'd proved her wrong.

Not long after, the women left and the man returned to his beer.

He'd been there for over an hour and Lacey hadn't flirted with him once. Unusual for Lacey who'd shucked inhibitions when she'd filed for divorce. Still, the opportunity had passed and flirting now would be a little too late and awkward.

It being a weeknight, the saloon closed at midnight, patrons filtering out one by one until the only customer left was the cowboy at the bar. Lacey had let him sit there even after the saloon closed because he was handsome, he'd made a girl's night and he looked as lonely as she felt. But the place was clean and the others would want to hit the road. No matter how good looking and nice, he had to leave.

Lacey sighed and leaned against the counter. "Sorry, cowboy, the bar is closed."

He glanced up, his brown eyes so dark they looked black in the dim lighting. "I didn't realize..." The man stood, settled his cowboy hat on his head and turned to leave.

"You can come back tomorrow," Lacey offered. "It beats spending your evening alone..." she added beneath her breath.

His gaze captured hers and a smile quirked the corners of his lips. "Might just do that, and you're right

—it beats being alone." The cowboy tipped his hat and left.

What was wrong with her tonight? Normally, Lacey would have flirted with the stranger and teased a smile out of him. But something had stopped her. Perhaps it was the way he'd kept to himself as if he wanted to be alone in a room full of people. More likely she'd steered clear because he was too good looking for his own good or hers. She had a hard time resisting a handsome face.

As her cowboy departed, Lacey sighed. So much for making it an interesting night. Instead of a one-night stand with a sexy hunk, she'd be going home to her empty apartment building.

"Place is clean enough. You ladies go home." Audrey Anderson, owner of the Ugly Stick Saloon, stood on her tiptoes, shoved the last bottle of whiskey onto the glass shelf behind the bar and lifted her strawberry-blond hair off the back of her neck. "Holy cow. Could it get any hotter? I can't wait to get home to a cool shower."

"And a hot cowboy?" Lacey quipped.

Jackson Gray Wolf was one of the hottest Kiowa cowboys in the county, next to his twin brothers, Mark and Luke. Audrey had sampled all three and only hinted at how great they were, before she claimed the oldest, Jackson. "He is pretty hot, isn't he?" Audrey grinned.

"Yeah." Lacey sighed, her mind on the last cowboy to leave the bar.

Audrey had Jackson waiting for her at home. Kendall had Ed Judson. Libby had Mark and Luke Gray Wolf and Isabella had the O'Brien brothers. Which left Lacey where?

Alone.

Lacey straightened her shoulders. Alone was better than married to an ass, which her ex had been.

"You gonna be all right?" Kendall Mason slipped an arm around Lacey's waist and squeezed. "I feel like I'm deserting you, leaving you all alone in the apartment building, and all."

Lacey pasted a smile on her face and hugged her friend. "Just remember, if you and Ed ever need a third to keep the sex education lessons rolling, I'm your gal." The offer was only superficial. Though she'd had sex with Kendall and Ed, she didn't want to cause any strife between the pair. They were perfect for each other all on their own.

"I'll keep that in mind." Kendall tugged the apron over her head and hung it on a hook. "I'm serious. You should stop by on your way home."

"No, sweetie. I wouldn't dream of horning in on your first night alone with Ed in your new house. Besides, Cory McBride is supposed to have moved into the apartment below mine today." Lacey smoothed a hand over her hair. "I need to give him a proper welcome."

"Lacey." Kendall shook her head. "Just remember, he's only twenty-one. A baby."

"Like you?" Lacey's lips quirked upward. "Old enough to be legal and young enough to have plenty of stamina. Besides, I'm only twenty-eight. Hardly a hag."

"You're by no means a hag. But don't scare the poor boy. We need him here on Ladies' Night. He draws a big crowd and he needs the tips to help pay for college.

Come to think of it, I haven't seen him date any of the women who hang out at the bar. He might not be into girls."

"Hot damn." Lacey clapped her hands together and rubbed them. "A challenge."

Kendall frowned. "I should have kept my mouth shut."

"Don't worry, Kendall, sweetheart. I won't wear the boy out...much." Lacey plumped her breasts and tugged up her cutoff jeans, showing a little more of her rounded derrière. "From the way the child dances, I'm sure he wouldn't mind a little more exercise. If he swings the other way, well then, no harm, no foul."

"Lacey, you crack me up. When are you going to find a man and settle down?"

Lacey's smile faded. "Honey, been there, done that, have scars to prove it. I'm thinking I might go for a woman next time. I have to admit, you were pretty damned tempting."

Kendall blushed. "You know that if I wasn't so into Ed, I'd be all over you."

"Thanks, hon, but you're the commitment type. You'd have me running screaming in the other direction. I'm all about having fun and no strings. You know me. Keep me hot and horny and the old biddies' tongues a-waggin' and I'm happy." After the women of the Temptation Garden Club had snubbed her, she loved yanking their chains. Her chest still ached when she thought about how cruel they'd been to her when she'd been in the right to divorce her cheating ex-husband.

Kendall patted Lacey's arm. "Someday you'll have to

get over what those old biddies did to you. They aren't worth gettin' your dander up over."

"I know. It still galls me that they were supposed to be my friends." Lacey sucked in a deep breath and pasted a smile on her face. "I'm fine now. Even better with the friends I've made at the Ugly Stick."

"Well, the offer's open if you wanna come over."

"Thanks, sweetie." Lacey's eyes misted.

"What happened with the cute cowboy at the bar?" Kendall waggled her brows. "With a little encouragement, he might have escorted you home."

"I didn't have time to flirt."

"Ha! You always flirt." Kendall crossed her arms.

Lacey shrugged. "He had a *do not disturb* sign written across his forehead."

"That never stopped you." Kendall's eyes narrowed. "You really aren't on your game."

"Go home." Lacey waved her hands at her friend. "Ed's bound to be naked waiting at the door for you."

Kendall grinned. "Yeah, he did that our last night in the apartment. God, he was cute. Guess I'd better get home before some ho bag finds him first." She hugged Lacey and sprinted out the back.

Lacey left before Audrey could corner her and give her the third degree about why she'd walked around all night down-in-the mouth and glum. Kendall and Ed's move from the apartment house to their new home had her in a funk so blue she couldn't seem to climb out. The empty apartment house reminded her of how alone she really was in Temptation, Texas.

Her foot barely tapped the gas as she crept home to

the empty house. Not until she pulled into the drive and parked next to Cory's convertible did she remember that she wouldn't be alone, if the new neighbor was still awake. And if the light burning in the window downstairs and the jumble of empty boxes stacked on the front porch were any indication, Cory was still up. If she hurried she could pop a frozen pizza in the microwave and be back down before he called it a night.

Cory was a little young for her, but any company tonight was better than going back to her apartment and being alone. Later, she'd break out her vibrator and satisfy that itch that had been growing since she'd let the hot cowboy at the bar go without coming on to him.

CHAPTER TWO

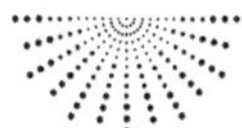

"*I*'m back." Nick McBride stepped through the front door of the tiny apartment, wondering how he'd ended up in such a mess. Until his house was finished, he was beholden to his little brother, Cory, for a temporary place to live.

He'd still be camped out on the greasy cot in the back of the auto-mechanic shop where he worked, if Cory hadn't offered to share his small apartment for the short-term. After they'd moved the big stuff into the apartment, Cory had suggested Nick run by the Ugly Stick Saloon and grab a beer. He'd certainly earned one.

Exhausted from moving what little he'd chosen to bring with him and all the items Cory had accumulated, Nick hadn't wanted to go anywhere but to bed. Cory insisted, saying he wanted some time to unpack a few things without bumping into his brother.

Nick had dragged himself to the saloon and ordered a beer. It was late on a weeknight and he was so tired he wanted to fall asleep on the barstool, but he stayed for over an hour, giving Cory time to make his apartment his own without big brother getting in his way. The waitresses at the Ugly Stick made him feel welcomed and had been a nice diversion from being alone with his thoughts. The one dance he'd participated in had lifted his spirits a little. But not much. The smile on the girl's face made him feel better, like maybe his life wasn't totally in the crapper.

"Are you as whipped as I am?" Cory stood at the refrigerator, a towel draped around his hips, his shoulder-length blond hair almost dry. "I totally forgot to pick up food."

"Everything is closed in Temptation." Nick's belly rumbled. "Guess we'll have to go hungry tonight."

"Mind looking at the AC tomorrow? I'm all thumbs when it comes to anything mechanical. And we can't go too long in this heat without some relief."

"I'll look at it in the morning." He didn't bother reminding his brother that he was a car mechanic, not an electrician. But Cory had always looked to him whenever something needed fixing.

Cory grinned over the fridge door. "We may not have any food in the place, but I have a six-pack of beer. Want one?"

"Maybe after I shower." Nick would rather have had a steak and baked potato, but maybe a cool beer might take the edge off his sore muscles and allow him to sleep better. He grabbed a towel out of a box and headed for the tiny bathroom. He stepped behind the shower curtain and turned on the cold water only, an image of the waitress leaning over the bar coming to mind.

She'd worn a flimsy, low-cut tank top and shorter-than-short blue jean cutoffs and boots. Her long dark hair had fallen around her shoulders in big loose curls. The kind a guy liked running his fingers through. The cool spray washed over him, barely doing the job of chilling his rising desires. If he hadn't been so out of practice, he might have spoken to her, maybe even asked her out. Hell, with his divorce so fresh, he wasn't sure he wanted to get back into the dating scene. So he'd sat there with his face practically buried in his beer mug, as the waitresses hurried back and forth, wasting an opportunity to get to know the one called Lacey.

Nick scrubbed his hair and body and rinsed off. When he stepped out of the shower and dried off, he felt better, more refreshed. The apartment was too hot with the AC out and he didn't feel like sweating in clean clothes, nor did he have to dress to impress anyone. Rather than slip into shorts or boxers, he stepped out of the bathroom with only the towel around his waist.

As soon as Nick exited the bathroom, Cory tossed him a long-neck bottle. "Think fast!"

Nick fumbled the catch but saved the bottle from hitting the old hardwood floor. He screwed off the top and tossed back his head, taking a long swallow. Then he dropped onto the couch, stretching his feet out in front of him. "God, it feels good to relax."

"Thanks for the loan of the furniture and the help moving it in." Cory sat at the other end of the couch and rested his feet on the coffee table. "I couldn't have done it without you."

"And I'd be sleeping at the shop. I owe you."

"Don't worry about it." Cory waved his hand. "You'll be back on track when the dust settles."

Nick snorted. "If Trish doesn't decide half of everything I owned wasn't enough."

Cory took another long swig of beer and let out a loud belch. "Your ex is a piece of work, isn't she?"

"She is."

"What happened? Why the divorce? You two were married for almost seven years."

Nick didn't feel like going into it. He'd spent too many hours with his lawyer, racking up a monumental attorney bill, and for what? Trish walked away with just about everything he owned, claiming he'd neglected her and that's why she had an affair. "It's a whole lot of horse shit."

"I get it, you don't want to talk about it. That's okay. If you need an ear, I'm here, otherwise, I won't ask."

"No, it's not that. It's—"

A loud beep interrupted Nick's explanation.

Cory sat up straight. "What the hell?"

"Sounds like a smoke detector." Nick said. "The battery probably wore out. Got a spare?"

Cory shook his head. "If I do, I wouldn't know which box to look in."

The alarm beeped again.

"Is it going to do that all night?" Cory asked.

"Most likely. It's a reminder to change the battery to keep you safe." Nick rose from the couch and followed the sound of the beep toward the front door of the apartment.

His brother followed. "How do we make it stop?"

"You have to disconnect it."

"I don't have a ladder and we didn't bring the chairs yet for the kitchen table. How the hell are we supposed to disconnect it?"

"I can give you a boost." Nick locked his fingers, cupped his hands and bent.

Cory stuck his foot in Nick's hands and reached for the alarm. He could barely grasp it enough to unhook it from the old building's high ceiling. "Got it."

"Now, pull the old battery out and leave the rest hanging until you can get another battery. And hurry it up, will ya? My fingers are slipping."

"Just a minute. The damned battery is being stubborn."

"I'm serious, I'm about to drop you." Nick swayed, his fingers slipping apart.

"Just…one…more…"

A knock on the door startled both men.

Nick lost his grip, Cory fell and both men landed on the floor as the door opened to the beautiful waitress from the Ugly Stick Saloon, wearing that breast-huggin white tank top, the shorter-than-short pair of jean cutoffs and bearing a tray filled with cheesy, gooey pizza.

She smiled, bent and scooped up both their towels, which had dropped loose when they'd fallen. Balancing the pizza tray with one hand and the towels looped over the other, she raised her eyebrows. "Having a little fun without me?"

Nick felt the heat rise from his chest into his face when he realized what this must look like. Cory lay draped across him in a highly suggestive position. At least he covered Nick's privates from the woman's view.

Cory laughed out loud. "Lacey, I wondered when you would show up. Kendall said you'd probably stop by to say hello."

"Did she?" Lacey's eyes narrowed. "What else did she say?"

Cory's grin broadened. "She said to watch out that you were on the prowl."

"She's a bigmouth, but since I'm here…" She waggled her eyebrows, her gaze panning over both men's groins. "Of course, if you're gay, maybe you can let me watch, or I'll pretend to be a boy and we can all have a little fun."

Nick choked and jumped to his feet, his hands forming a fig leaf over his crotch.

Cory chortled. "Ah, Lacey, nothing like cutting to the chase. We were just trying to kill the smoke detector and fell."

Lacey pouted. "Well, darn." Her gaze went to Nick, sliding down his chest to where his hands covered his privates.

"Do you mind?" Nick held out his hand for a towel, the heat her gaze generated pooling in his groin.

"A shame to cover something so fine." She grinned and tossed him the towel. "So, are you interested?"

In her? Hell yeah. She hadn't been off his mind since

he'd walked into the Ugly Stick Saloon earlier. Nick grabbed the towel and slung it around his hips. Standing naked in front of her had thrown him off-balance and he wasn't certain how to get back on an even keel. "I don't know…"

"It's a meat-lover's pizza." She stood there with her nipples puckered beneath the shirt, her brows raised in challenge. "Unless pizza's not your thing…" She turned as if to leave, throwing a wink over her shoulder.

A groan rose up Nick's throat. Damn, she was as cute and as sassy as she'd been at the saloon earlier when he'd had a hard time keeping his eyes off her. Nick felt as if he stood on quicksand, the floor sucking at his feet. His cock hardened at the sight of the brunette's luscious curves, his gaze running from the narrowing of her waist to the ragged hem of the cutoffs, displaying the rounded curve of her ass.

"Nick might not be interested, but as far as I'm concerned, I love pizza." Cory lunged forward, his muscles rippling, six-pack taut, his long pale-blond hair drying in big loose curls around his shoulders, like a friggin' Greek God, drying in the sun. He grabbed her around the middle and spun her around, reaching for the pizza tray.

Lacey laughed. "Easy there, I almost lost it." She steadied the tray.

Nick's gut tightened. He fought the urge to yank his brother back and take Lacey…er, the pizza…all for himself. Before he could move on the urge, Cory snatched the pizza from Lacey's hands and dove in like a starving man. "I'd do just about anything for a bite of pizza."

Lacey's hand rested on her sexy hip and her lips twisted. "Wow, that really hits a girl right in the ego."

"No offense, Lacey," Cory said between chews. "It's just that I haven't eaten since breakfast."

Lacey tossed Cory his towel and turned toward Nick. "Aren't you going to introduce me to your friend?"

Cory swallowed. "Oh, he's not my friend, Nick's my brother. He'll be rooming with me while he's waiting—"

"Until I can find a house." Nick tightened the towel firmly around his middle, appalled at the way it tented over his dick. He hoped Lacey wouldn't notice.

"Pizza first?" Her gaze moved from his cock to his face. "Then whatever?"

"Pizza sounds great." He wasn't that desperate that he'd fall into bed with the first woman who came along after his divorce was final. No matter that she had all the right equipment and plenty of it, and that she was drop-dead gorgeous and she seemed interested in doing more than eating pizza with both him and Cory. His head was screaming *Whoa!* His cock told him something entirely different.

Cory dropped the pizza tray on top of a box doubling as a coffee table and waved at the couch. "Have a seat."

Lacey eased onto the couch, tucked her legs beneath her and reached for a slice of pizza.

Nick chose to sit on the chair facing the couch, as far from the temptress as he could get and not be rude.

Something about her teasing look, her sultry brown eyes and the swell of her breasts beneath her shirt had him all in a knot.

He nearly choked on his first bite of gooey cheese and crust, timed perfectly with Lacey lifting a slice of pizza to her lips. Her nipples tightened behind the near-sheer fabric of her tank top, her pale rosy brown aureoles barely visible in the soft lighting, like hints of round slices of tasty Canadian bacon.

Nick tried to keep his attention on the slice of pizza pie in his hand, but his gaze strayed toward Lacey again and again.

When she dropped a slice of pepperoni and it landed in her cleavage, Nick almost came.

"Oops." She grinned. "I'm such a mess."

"May I?" Cory leaned across and plucked the morsel from her skin.

A soft, sweet laugh bubbled up from Lacey's throat. "Um, that tickles. Be sure to get enough to eat. A growing boy like you needs his strength."

"Just so you know, I'm no virgin." Cory bit into another slice of pizza. "Kendall said you could still teach me a few things. I make a good student."

The bite Nick had just taken lodged in his throat. He swallowed hard, nearly gagging on the wad of crust.

Lacey licked a string of cheese from her lips. "You don't mind learning from an older woman?"

"You're hardly older than me, and I think older women rock at sex."

Nick groaned. All the talk about sex had him harder than a fence post. Why he should be concerned about

Lacey and his brother having sex was beyond him. Hell, Lacey wasn't much older than his little brother. Still a woman as sultry and sexy as Lacey deserved a man old enough to know what foreplay was and what made a woman scream.

Like him.

Nick bit into the pizza and choked it down. According to his ex-wife, he'd failed in the sack. Hell, she'd never wanted to have sex when they were together. Apparently, she'd been getting enough without him.

After shooting a sassy grin at Nick, Lacey returned her attention to Cory. "What does a boy still wet behind the ears have to offer?"

Cory grinned. "Kendall taught me some dance moves that never fail to get the ladies hot."

"I've seen those hips move at Ladies' Night out. I might be convinced to trade a dance for a sex lesson. If you're good enough."

Cory glanced at Nick. "Sorry old man. Is this conversation making you uncomfortable?"

Hell yes it was. Nick swallowed another bite of pizza. "No, not at all," he lied. "Knock yourselves out."

His brother tipped his head toward Nick. "Nick's probably not interested in participating, but I'm game, if you are."

Nick almost blew pizza chunks out his nose. Not interested? His body wanted her, even if his mind was against it. He ended up coughing for the next minute.

Lacey rounded the table and stood next to him, patting his back. "Are you all right?"

With Lacey beside him, her breast rubbing his naked shoulder, her sexy cutoffs brushing his fingertips, Nick was far from all right.

Meanwhile, Lacey spoke to Cory across Nick's shoulder. "I thought you were worn out."

"That was hunger talking." Cory patted his six-pack. "I'm recharged and ready to go." He dropped the crust onto the tray and hurried to the stereo system, connecting wires and plugging it into the wall. Before long a raunchy bump-and-grind song blared through the speakers. Cory crossed the room, rocking his hips, his cock jutting out beneath the towel.

Nick set his pizza aside, unable to eat while the heat was ratcheting up and the walls were closing in around Cory and Lacey.

Cory swung the lounge chair out in the middle of the small room and guided Lacey to it, pressing her onto the cushioned surface.

"Oh, so you're going to give me the treatment, are you?" Lacey leaned back, her eyes dancing. "Bring it on, little man."

"I'll show you little." He whipped the towel from around his waist and dangled his cock in her face.

She laughed and ran a finger along his thick shaft. "I stand corrected."

Nick sat dumbstruck in his chair as his younger brother danced around their guest like a professional stripper. Holy hell. Cory had told him he'd been dancing for tips at the Ugly Stick and bachelorette parties, but Nick had never seen him actually perform.

At one point Cory sat his ass in her lap, then leaned

over to touch his toes, his balls hanging loose between his legs. "Spank me, Lacey."

"This night is turning out better than I could have hoped for." Lacey spanked his buttocks.

"That the best you can do?" Cory teased. "I thought older women had this trick down." He shook his ass in her face.

She slapped Cory hard, leaving a red print on his cheek.

Nick's dick hardened, and his butt muscles clenched each time Lacey slapped his brother's ass.

"Better." He danced out of her reach, turned toward her and danced back, his cock sticking straight out, bobbing in time to his moves.

Nick turned away, his dick so tight it ached. "I think I'll go to bed and leave you two to it."

"Party pooper." Lacey waved him toward her. "Don't you want to show the whelp what a real man can do?"

He frowned. "I'm not into threesomes."

"How do you know?" she challenged, her gaze slipping to the telltale evidence of his interest. "Ever been in one?"

His shoulders straightened, his chin tipping up. "No, and I don't plan on starting."

Cory danced around her then spun off and gyrated around Nick. "Ah, come on, bro, don't disappoint the lady."

"I don't need this. I'm not ready."

Cory snorted, his gaze going to the giant tent Nick's dick was making beneath the towel. "Really?"

With his brother's dick bobbing toward him, Nick

was beginning to think moving in with Cory might not have been such a good idea. What kind of ideas had he gotten from stripping at the Ugly Stick? "I don't have sex with just anyone."

"Lighten up, big brother." Cory turned to face the woman in the chair. "Lacey's not just anyone."

"I believe sex should be shared with someone you are committed to." And he sure as hell wasn't ready to commit to anyone in the near future. Not after he'd been burned so badly.

Lacey snorted. "Then definitely, go to bed. I'm not the commitment type. All I want is a little harmless sex with two good-looking men. But one will do."

"Thanks." Cory shook his head. "Way to shoot a boner down."

"Sorry, sweetcakes." Lacey stood and grabbed his cock, massaging it back to a full head. "It's only fair that you know the truth up front. I'm not here for a happily ever after." She shot a glance over her shoulder, her gaze directed at Nick. "I don't believe in them."

A surge of disappointment made Nick cross his arms over his chest. "Good, because neither do I."

Lacey's brows rose. "Good."

"Good." Nick's nod was curt, intended to end the conversation. At that point he should have stalked off to his bedroom. But he didn't.

"Well that's one thing we can agree on." Lacey let go of Cory's dick and closed the distance between her and Nick. "Now, are you going to use that thing or slink off to the bathroom for a cold shower?"

His eyes narrowed the closer she got. "I've already had my shower."

"Then don't be shy." She grabbed his towel and yanked it free of his hips. She studied him, turning him to the side, her head tipped. "Um. Passable."

Sassy, wasn't she? Nick frowned, his chest pushing out. "What do you mean passable?"

"I've seen guys with big dicks and the poor fellas didn't know what to do with them."

"I know what to do," Nick ground out.

She touched his cock with the tip of her finger, dropping her voice into a soft, sultry drawl Nick was sure she'd used to seduce other men. "Then show me, big fella."

Nick growled, his blood humming through his veins, lust wreaking havoc with what little was left of his control. "Woman, you've about pushed all my buttons."

She skimmed her hand over his length all the way to his balls. "As long as one of them was the on switch."

Unable to resist a moment longer, he scooped her up in his arms and carried her toward the bedroom and the mattress still lying on the floor.

Cory stood in the middle of the living room, his shoulders sagging. "Does that mean I don't get a lesson?"

Lacey leaned up over Nick's shoulder. "No, that means, come on, we're gonna rumble!"

Cory started forward.

Nick growled again. "I didn't say I'd be party to a ménage."

The younger McBride ground to a halt. "So, what's it to be? Am I in or out?"

Lacey leaned back in Nick's arms and stared up at him. "If Cory isn't invited, you can put me down. I want both of you, and if I can't have what I want, I'll take my pizza and go home."

"Damn your pizza." For a long moment, he stared down at her. Then his shoulders rose and fell and he flung a look over his shoulder. "The lady wants you too."

"A good thing. That's my bed you're aiming for."

Nick groaned again. Damn this entire situation. He'd get in for a good fuck and send this broad back to her apartment. No strings, no *call me later*…nothing. In and out and that would be the end of it.

What was it he'd learned in college literature? Best laid plans of mice and men…

Nick soon learned that Lacey had other plans and a quick in and out wasn't one of them.

CHAPTER THREE

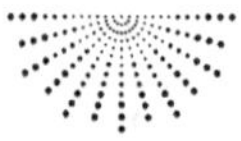

After a rocky start, Lacey was well on her way to scratching her itch with not one but two handsome men. Life didn't get better. So what if one of them frowned like a grizzly with a sore paw. He had a cock that could make a horse blush, and she was about to get some of it.

And if the old biddies of the Temptation Garden Club got wind of her ménage with a couple of guys living in the same house as she was, all the better.

She'd come down the stairs with low to no expectations of getting laid, but once she set eyes on Nick, the guy she'd been drooling over at the Ugly Stick, her hopes grew, as did Nick's magnificent cock.

The man was tall and broad shouldered, with wavy, dark hair that hung long around his ears. He had that slightly weathered look of a man who had a little bit of life experience. It was far past sexy and had her body humming with desire.

The two men might be brothers, but they were as different as night and day. Cory with his long silky mane of white-blond hair and blue eyes and Nick with his unruly dark locks and deep brown eyes. Yum.

Lacey knew Cory, and wouldn't mind a bit of play with the gorgeous stripper, but Nick…

Now, there was a real man.

She expected him to lay her on the mattress, instead, he tossed her.

Lacey squealed, landing with a soft thump, her pulse quickening with the little bit of rough play.

Nick pointed a finger at her. "Get this straight. No strings."

She nodded, letting her lips curl into a sassy, sexy smile. "That's my rule in any relationship. No strings."

"I'm not going to call you tomorrow, so don't bother waiting by the phone."

"No phone." She leaned up on her elbows and stroked her finger over her jean-clad crotch. "You're making me wet with anticipation, cowboy."

"And I'm only doing this ménage thing once." He glanced down at his stiff erection. "Because if I don't, I'm going to hurt all night long."

She scrambled to her knees and reached up to stroke his cock. "Can't have you hurtin', now, can we?" She cupped his balls and guided his dick to her lips. "I know just the thing to make you feel better. In fact, I think I can cure you."

"No woman will ever cure me."

"Into boys, are you?" She dropped her voice to a low

tenor. "I can pretend to be a boy, if that's what gets you off."

Cory snorted behind her. "I don't think that's what he meant. But that might be fun."

Lacey stuck out her tongue and licked a circle around the head of Nick's cock. "You can pull my hair if you like. I like it a little rough."

"Hot damn." Cory scooted around Nick, his cock brushing against Nick's hip.

The older man shook his head. "I'm not into boys."

"Well, brother, I'm not into boys either, but if the lady wants both of us, I'm willing." Cory grinned.

"Blah, blah, blah." Lacey rolled her eyes. "All talk, no action and I'll be on my way home to my trusty vibrator." She licked Nick's cock again, this time trailing her tongue down to the base.

His member twitched.

She smiled. "Like that?"

He moaned. "God, that feels good,"

"Been too long?" she quizzed.

His lips twisted. "Way too long." There was a story behind his words.

Lacey was curious, but too hot to delve deeper at that moment. The dark, smoky-eyed look he gave her made her tingle all over. "Bet you want it hard and fast."

"I want it any way I can get it."

"Talk like that will go to a girl's head." She licked his head. "I'm beginning to feel like a freak being the only one who's not naked." Lacey raised her arms. When Nick didn't move, she rolled her eyes. "That was a hint."

Nick snatched the hem of her tank top and ripped it

up over her head. His breath caught and his eyes flared, his gaze on the rounded swells of her breasts.

Lacey's nipples tightened into tight little buds. She wanted him to take one into his mouth and suck hard. But he seemed a bit reluctant to initiate anything. "That's a start." Her fingers went to the button at the waistband of her shorts.

Nick brushed her hands aside, flipped the rivet through the hole and slid the zipper down, pushing aside the lace of her thong panties. The man groaned when his hand skimmed across her thatch of curly brown hair. His cock pulsed and his hands shook.

Lacey's hopes rose. If his visible physical reactions were anything to go on, she had his interest, even it was given reluctantly.

When the shorts and panties reached her knees where they were buried in the mattress, Nick pushed her gently back against the comforter and straightened her legs, tugging the shorts off her ankles.

As soon as Nick slung her jean shorts to the floor, Lacey sprang back to her knees, her breasts bobbing in Nick's face. After his dogged denial to participate, Lacey was even more determined to push Nick's boundaries. And having both men in the room helped with her initial shyness over flirting with the brooding cowboy, emboldening her every move. She glanced over Nick's shoulder at Cory. "Ever done it doggy-style, college boy?"

Cory shrugged. "Sadly, my education has not included that particular position…yet."

"Then step right up." She came up on her hands and

knees and waggled her ass, so hot she thought she might self-combust before she got the ball rolling. "I'm wet and ready, whenever you are."

"You're killing me, woman," Nick said through clenched teeth.

"I plan on doing a whole lot more to you before you die, cowboy. So hang around." She took him full into her mouth, sucking hard, dragging him all the way to bump against the back of her throat.

His fingers threaded through her hair and he moaned. "Holy hell, that feels good."

Lacey dragged her teeth across his velvety-smooth cock as she eased out to the tip. "Thought you'd like that."

Cory dropped to his knees behind her on the mattress.

"Know your way around back there, college boy?" she asked.

He laughed. "I think I can find the spot."

"Then do it. I'm already halfway there." She glanced back at him. "And I like to be spanked."

Cory smacked her ass with his young, big hand. "Like that?"

"I've had love pats harder than that. Try again and, this time, make it count." She raised her ass higher.

He slapped her hard enough that the sting made her flinch, and the burning sensation against her naked bottom almost made her come right then. "Oh, yeah. You are a quick learner." She glanced up at Nick. "Well? Are you going to let Cory show you how it's done? I've already told you I like to have my hair pulled. Do I have to tell you how to do that?"

Nick's eyes narrowed as his fingers wove through her hair. At first hesitant, he finally gave in and gave her head a little shove, angling her toward his dick. "You want it rough, I'll give you rough." He pushed hard enough to force her face close. "Suck it, woman."

"Now, that's more like it."

"A little less talk." He reached low and pinched the tip of her nipple. "A little more suction."

"Mmmm. Yes sir, cowboy." Balancing on one hand, she cupped his balls and slid her mouth over his dick, reveling in how thick and hard it was.

His hands tightened in her hair, forcing her to take all of him. He pumped in and out of her mouth, his hips settling into a rhythmic motion.

Then Cory's hand smoothed over her rump, finding the crease between her cheeks and following it down to the tight little hole of her anus. "If I was into guys, this is where I'd go." He poked his thumb into her ass.

Lacey gasped around Nick's cock. "Don't let the fact that I'm a girl stop you."

Nick pulled her hair and forced her attention back to him while Cory explored her other end, his fingers slipping into her channel.

She couldn't think of a more titillating experience. Her ex had never been one to play and try something new. Missionary-style, wham-bam and he was done.

But this…

Her belly tightened, a rush of sensations flowing to

her core, lubricating her pussy as Cory swirled his finger around her entrance.

"You are wet, sweetheart. Want me to fuck you?" Cory asked.

"Yes," she said, her mouth full of cock.

"Say the magic word," Cory teased.

Lacey pulled free of Nick's cock. "Oh, for Pete's sake do it, before I explode. Please."

Nick held his body rigid, his hands in Lacey's hair. "Are you sure this isn't too much?"

"Oh, darlin' I can take it. And I trust you not to hurt me." She glanced up at him. "Pull my hair?"

Nick's fingers tightened and he tugged her back to his cock, a frown creasing his forehead. "This is all so new."

"But fun, right?" Cory positioned his cock at her entrance, his finger pumping in and out, preparing her for bigger and better things.

She spread her legs wider, offering herself.

Cory grabbed her hips and thrust into her. "I can't hold back."

"Don't," Lacey said around Nick's thickness.

"Wait." Nick leaned over, pulling free of Lacey's mouth, and rummaged in the nightstand. When he straightened, he tossed a foil packet to Cory.

Cory tore open the packet and slipped the condom over his dick.

Lacey rewarded Nick with a gentle squeeze on his balls as she sucked him back into her mouth. Not only was Nick sexy, he was a gentleman, and thought of protection when she was too into the moment for her brain to engage.

"Damn, woman, you're hot," Cory moaned. He pumped in and out of her, alternating between poking a finger in her ass and slapping her bottom.

The sting of Nick's hands pulling on her hair and the assault on her cunt had her rising quickly to the peak, pitching her over into a cataclysmic orgasm. Her body shuddered and her eyes closed as she savored the impact.

NICK'S BREATH caught as he witnessed his little brother sliding his cock into the woman giving him a blow job. He nearly shot his wad that very second. He'd never thought he'd get off on a ménage. But here he was hotter than he'd ever been in his life. It had been over ten months since he'd had sex, and he was coming too fast. Even when he was married, sex hadn't been often. His ex was never in the mood.

She'd divorced him based on neglect, stating she'd been left too often by herself, while he worked late at the shop or out on their little ranch. Not until the divorce was final had he discovered she was having an affair. No wonder she hadn't wanted sex. She'd been getting it from the neighbor's gardener all along.

He was so ready to come as Lacey swallowed his penis over and over. A man wasn't meant to go that long without sex. Masturbation in the shower only got him so far. A real fucking was what he needed.

With his fingers clenched in her hair, tingles spread

throughout his body, his groin tightened, and his cock swelled so hard it hurt. Nick held himself in check by the slimmest thread of control. The woman was so damned sexy, he could easily lose it.

When Lacey's body stilled and her fingers clutched his balls a little too snugly, he could tell she'd reached her climax. Nick refused to release. He wanted what Cory was having, his cock buried deep in Lacey's pussy.

Cory slammed in once more and remained buried for a full minute before pulling free. "Wow, Lacey. You're amazing." Cory scooted away and fell onto his back. "I'm all in."

Nick tugged Lacey's hair, pulling her off him. "I'm not. Are you?"

Lacey stared up at him, her mouth curving. "Not hardly. Want me to play sub to your dom? I could get into a little BDSM. How about you?"

He frowned. "I have no idea what you're talking about."

"You can be the master. I'll do whatever you tell me. If I don't, you can punish me." She waggled her brows.

"You trust me to do that?"

"I wouldn't ask you if I didn't trust you." She smiled up at him. "Now, are you game?"

His frown deepened. "If you're sure."

"I'm sure."

"Oh, this is rich. Big brother getting into BDSM. I never thought I'd see the day." Cory folded his arms behind his head. "Nick, you've got a tiger by the tail with that one." The younger man rolled over and retrieved a necktie from a stack of clothes on the floor. "Here, start with this." He handed Nick the tie.

Nick stared at the tie. "What am I supposed to do with this?"

"Really?" Cory laughed. "Tie her up. That's what you want, isn't it, Lacey?"

"I've been very bad." She touched a finger to her lip. "I might run away." She inched toward the edge of the bed, trailing a fingernail along Nick's length. "I've had some very naughty thoughts about fucking in front of an open window where all the old biddies of town can see."

Nick's eyes widened. "Are you kidding me?" The image emblazoned on his mind of Lacey cavorting in front of the open window made his cock even harder.

"See? I'm very bad." Lacey winked at him. "I should go before I act on those thoughts." She slipped off the bed, her breasts bouncing saucily.

Nick couldn't let her go, not with a hard-on to beat all hard-ons. He grabbed her wrist and looped the tie around it. "No. You have to stay and see this through."

"Is that an order?" she challenged.

Nick glanced at Cory. When the younger man nodded, Nick forced steel into his voice. "Yes. That's an order." Then he whispered. "If at any time you think it's too much, just tell me. I don't want to hurt you."

"Yes, master." She ducked her head, her hand sliding over her belly to her pussy. "I've been bad for fornicating with another man in your presence. What is my punishment, master?"

"Tie her to the bed," Cory suggested, then added,

"On the side nearest to the window. Mrs. Biedel, in the house next door, likes to snoop. When I was taking dance lessons from Kendall, the old lady had it spread around town that I was paying her for sex."

Nick's brows rose. "I can't do that to Lacey. Think of the rumors that will get started."

Lacey's hand cupped her crotch, a finger slipping between her own folds. "Rumors about me make me hotter. Consider it a favor, master."

"Quiet, woman," Nick barked, trying to think with his head, not his dick. "And stop doing that with your finger. It's making me nuts."

"Yes, master." She tipped her head downward, a secret smile curling her lips as she lifted her finger from her clit to pinch her nipple.

Nick groaned. "Fine!" He bound her wrist with the necktie and secured it to the headboard on the side closest to the window. "Lie on the bed."

"Yes, master." She dropped onto the bed.

Her naked body made Nick's cock twitch in anticipation of what would come next. The game she was playing had his blood burning through his veins. He'd never forced himself on a woman. His ex had never wanted to play...with him. But Lacey...

The woman had more gall than a whore on the street corner and it brought out the beast in him.

Cory rolled off the bed and shoved the mattress closer to the open window. "That ought to raise the old woman's blood pressure."

"Hmmm. And she's a member of the Temptation Garden Club." Lacey purred. "Perfect." Her knees dropped to the sides, exposing her lush, wet pussy to Nick. "Are you going to fuck me?"

"Need help holding her down?" Cory lifted Lacey, slid behind her back and reached beneath her legs, pulling her knees up, spreading her even wider. "How's that?"

Nick was beginning to think he'd gotten into something way over his head, but he couldn't walk away. Not now. No way. "Yes, hold her. She deserves punishment and I plan to give it to her." Question was how? "Geez it's hot in here." If Nick could loosen his collar, he would. But he was naked.

"I'm on fire," Lacey moaned. Her hand reached down to caress her clit.

"There's a few long-necks left in the fridge." Cory nodded to Nick. "Maybe she'd like a drink."

Nick stepped away from the bed and took the few steps into the kitchen to grab the beer from the fridge, the coolness of the bottle bringing him back to his senses. Almost.

At that point, he should have run. But his cock led him back to the bedroom where Cory still held Lacey's legs back and her pussy glistened in the light from the lamp.

Nick twisted the top from the bottle and took a long draw, hoping the cool liquid would temper his own heat.

Then he held the bottle to Lacey's lips. "Drink."

She wrapped her lips around the bottle like she'd wrapped her lips around his cock.

Nick's hand shook as he tipped the bottle, pouring a

generous swig into her mouth. A small amount trickled out the side of her mouth and down her neck.

His gaze followed the trail of the beer as it dribbled between her breasts. He bent to tongue the drop.

Her chest rose up and she twisted to the side, presenting a taut nipple for his mouth to consider, ripe and full like vine-ripened fruit.

Nick couldn't resist. He took a bite, nibbling on the hardened tip, rolling it between his teeth and flicking it with his tongue. God, she tasted sweet.

Her free hand captured his balls and squeezed. "What would you like to do to me, master?"

Slipping into the fantasy wholeheartedly, Nick replied in a deep voice, "Fuck you like a whore."

"Geez, Nick, could you be a little more crass." Cory chuckled.

"Umm." Lacey slid her tongue across her lips.

Nick swallowed the last of the beer and reached out to set the bottle on the floor, but at the last minute changed his mind, dirty thoughts sprouting like seeds in his head.

He trailed a finger from her bellybutton to the thatch of hair covering her sex, then parted her folds, exposing the nubbin of her desire. With a flick, he tapped her clit.

Lacey gasped, her ass rising off the mattress, her thighs straining against Cory's hold. "Oh, master, please...do it again."

Nick flicked it again.

Lacey moaned, closing her eyes.

Nick slapped her thigh, gently. "Eyes open," he

demanded. He liked how dark Lacey's brown eyes got each time he touched her.

Her eyes popped open, her breathing growing more tortured. "Hurry. I'm so close."

He puffed out his chest. "I'll do as I please." A few minutes ago, he'd have been appalled at his words. Nick was amazed how quickly he was getting into the master-slave thing, much faster than he'd thought possible.

Cory chuckled. "Nice, Nick."

Nick turned the beer bottle upside down, letting the last of the alcohol drip onto Lacey's clit.

Her chest rose and fell on a silent gasp. "Sweet. You're getting the hang of it." Her voice practically purred.

Nick's cock twitched. He wanted to drive into her and fuck her until she screamed, but first he wanted her to want him as badly as he wanted her.

Still holding the chilled bottle, he slid it across the drops of beer.

Her gaze followed the long-neck's path as he slid it lower, to swirl it around the opening to her wet, glistening pussy.

Making her hot was igniting Nick into an inferno, but he held his own raging desires in check as he built on Lacey's.

Lacey leaned forward, her glance glued to what he was doing with the bottle. "Are you going to…"

"I am." He pressed the mouth of the bottle into her cunt, sliding it easily into her slick channel.

Lacey leaned back against Cory's chest, her eyes rolling upward. "So cool…so fucking hot."

He pulled it out.

She lifted her head and wailed, "Don't stop!"

"Are you demanding?" Nick slapped her thigh, hard enough to leave a red mark like Cory had, feeling a little stab of guilt that he might be hurting her.

She flinched, her tongue snaking out to moisten her lips, her eyes flaring at the punishment. Clearly Lacey was true to her word and liked it a little rough. She sucked in a breath and whispered, "No."

Nick sucked in air and forced himself to say, "Who is the master?"

Her mouth curved into a little smile that had Nick's gut knotting. "You are."

"Then ask me…the right way." He held the bottle close to her pussy, but refused to insert it until she played along.

"Oh, please, master. Please do it again."

He hesitated a moment more, prolonging her torture, before he slid it into her and back out again.

Each time he pushed the bottle in, her head rose up, her body tightened and she held her breath.

After a few more pumps with the bottle, Nick had her where he wanted her, on the verge of orgasm. She wanted him as badly as he wanted her.

He pulled the bottle out and set it on the floor.

"Wait, please, master…I want more." She struggled against Cory's hold.

"I don't know what you're planning, but I can't hold

her much longer." Cory grunted, his hands slipping along Lacey's thigh.

"You can let go." Nick was ready to finish what he'd started. After ten months, he'd have his release and Lacey would know just who was the master. He slid a condom over his engorged cock.

Cory let go of Lacey's thighs and scooted out from beneath her.

Before Lacey could reach for the tie binding her to the bed, Nick positioned her thighs over his shoulders. His knees dug into the mattress as he plunged deep into Lacey's cunt.

Her heat surrounded him, the muscles of her channel clenching around his engorged cock. For a moment he savored the feel of her. Then he was slamming in and out like a racehorse pounding toward the finish line.

"Yes!" Lacey cried out. "Yes!" She dragged in a deep breath and let it out slowly on a moan.

Beyond endurance, Nick thrust one more time, held for an agonizingly exquisite release. When his cock stopped throbbing, he sat back on his heels, breathing hard as he eased Lacey's legs to each side of him. For a moment, he stared down at the apex of her thighs, amazed by the intensity of his release. He traced a line from her clit to her dripping pussy. "That was incredible."

Cory stood at the open window. "Yeah, and Old Lady Biedel is glaring out her window."

Lacey grinned. "Good. My work here is done." She

caressed Nick's flagging shaft and smiled up at him. "Thanks for a good time." She climbed to her feet, swaying slightly, then crossed to Cory where she stood naked in full view of the open window and kissed the boy, her hands sliding down over his ass. "You two aren't bad. Perhaps I'll consider a replay. We'll see." She stooped to retrieve her shorts, then she sauntered out of the room, her hips swaying, her dark brown hair swinging down to her waist.

Nick wanted to stop her, to go for round two right then. He stood and took a step toward her.

Cory grabbed his arm. "Let her go."

A burst of anger shot through Nick. He didn't want her to go. He wanted her to stay through the night. He shook off his brother's hold and took another step, bringing him to the threshold between the bedroom and the living-room-kitchen combo.

Lacey bent to grab her tank top from the floor where she'd dropped it.

Her curvy ass beckoned to Nick, making him want to take her from behind, to fuck her like there was no tomorrow.

"She told you she didn't want strings," Cory reminded him.

Oh yeah. Hadn't he said the same? "Neither do I," he muttered, less convinced now than he'd been an hour ago.

With Lacey there might not be a tomorrow.

And that bothered Nick more than he cared to admit.

CHAPTER FOUR

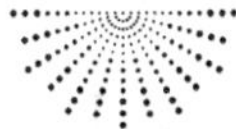

*L*acey slept like a baby through what was left of
the night and awoke to sunshine, blue skies and
a heart lighter than it had been since she'd come
to Temptation five years ago.

A knock at her door had her tossing back the covers
and running to answer. Maybe the boys…er…men
downstairs had come for a second helping. She was up
for it.

"Just a minute!" Lacey called out.

She finger-combed her hair with quick strokes, ran a
quick toothbrush over her teeth, then raced from the
bathroom to throw open the door, wearing a smile and
nothing else.

Kendall's brows rose and her mouth twisted as she
fought a smile. "Oh, baby, glad you didn't feel the need
to get dressed on my account."

A stab of disappointment made Lacey glance around
Kendall and look toward the staircase.

"Nope. No one behind me. Ed had to work today and no one's home in the apartment below." Kendall's brows dipped. "What did you do last night?" Her eyes widened. "You did Cory."

"Relax." A trace of heat rose up Lacey's neck and into her cheeks. "I didn't just pick on Cory."

"What do you mean?"

"Cory has a roommate." Lacey spun away, hugging herself around her middle. "Isn't it a glorious day?" She flung out her arms and floated toward the window, yanking on the shade, sending it spinning up into the roll. Then she opened the window and leaned out, naked and loving it. "I fucked two men last night and it was fabulous!"

Kendall followed Lacey into the apartment and closed the door behind her. "Uh, Lacey, I'm not certain, but I think there are laws about indecent exposure."

"I don't give a rat's ass about laws. I had the best sex ever last night."

"Who's Cory's roommate?" Kendall asked.

Lacey smiled over her shoulder, her body warming all over. "His big brother."

"Nick? The incredibly hot cowboy mechanic?" Kendall's eyes narrowed. "Wasn't that him at the bar late last night?"

"Yes." With a big sigh, Lacey grabbed a shirt and slipped it over her head, then dropped onto the sofa and sat Indian-style, her fingers cupping her pussy, still sensitive from making love to both men last night and wet again at just the memory. "Shoot, Kendall, I haven't felt this good since the year I came to Temptation all starry-eyed and in love with my first husband."

"Careful, Lacey. That didn't end so great."

Lacey shrugged. "No, last night was sooo much better. This time I wasn't a young newlywed dreaming of living here happily ever after, raising children and being a contributing member of the elite Temptation Garden Club." That dream had only lasted for about a year, and for the two years following, she'd lived in misery, wondering what she'd done wrong to make Randy lose interest in her. It took gossiping, so-called friends of the Temptation Garden Club to set her straight and show her that it wasn't her at all, but that beyotch, Desiree Donnelly, who'd siphoned off all of Randy's sexual desire. "No, this was uncommitted, purely carnal, no-holds-barred sex with a little BDSM thrown in for good measure." She closed her eyes, recalling how good it had felt to have two men making her so hot she could have exploded like fireworks on the Fourth of July. "And I'll bet you dollars to donuts, Old Lady Biedel got an ear and eye full of it all."

Kendall snorted. "Her and that snooty bunch of garden witches were never anything to write home about. I can't believe they stuck up for your ex when he was the one cheating on *you*. And they had the gall to blame you for your husband's infidelity."

"Yeah." Lacey smiled dreamily. "It won't be long before that old witch flaps her gums about how Cory and Nick fucked my brains out. Maybe she'll get a hint of what she's missing and wish she was me for once."

Just when she'd needed the support of friends, Lacey

had learned the hard way that the ladies of the garden club were only fair-weather friends. As soon as divorce was mentioned, they blamed Lacey for her husband's infidelity and shunned her. Abandoned and heartbroken, Lacey lost the battle in divorce court—thanks to a corrupt judge and a crappy attorney—and found herself out of her home, out of money and friendless.

Until Audrey Anderson, the owner of the Ugly Stick Saloon, took her under her wing and gave her hope for her future and a reason to keep going when she had nothing and no one.

"Yeah, I feel better than I've felt since I arrived in Temptation, and it all has to do with Nick…and Cory." Nick in particular, but Lacey wasn't willing to say that out loud. Somehow that made it too personal and she'd sworn off getting too personal.

Kendall sat across from her, her gaze drifting to where Lacey was rubbing her clit. She squirmed in her chair and her tongue snaked out across her bottom lip. "It's like I said, you needed a man of your own— Holy hell, Lacey, will you stop already? You're making me horny just watching."

Lacey winked. "Wanna play around a little for old time's sake?"

Kendall shook her head, her gaze still glued to Lacey's hand covering her clit. "No, Ed and I are perfectly happy."

"Invite him over. Surely he can afford to take a lunch break to please his woman." Lacey closed her eyes, sucking in a sharp breath. Already her pussy ached. "Oh, yeah. Call him. I could stand to live a little vicariously now."

"Damn it, Lacey, you're making me hot just looking at you."

The sounds of keys jingling and articles shifting made Lacey open her eyes.

Kendall rifled through her purse and jerked out her cell phone, punching at the speed-dial button. "Ed?"

Lacey grinned. She'd helped the pair explore each other's bodies and break the best-friend barrier to enjoy hot, raw sex. "Tell him his services are needed," she urged.

"Wanna have sex?" Kendall purred into the phone. She paused. "Now, for heaven's sake!" Her free hand slipped inside the waistband of her jeans. "What's wrong with your truck? I see. You don't mind if Lacey and I start without you? That's what I thought. God, I love you. I'll be hot and ready when you get here. Where? Oh, I'm at Lacey's. Okay. Smooches." She kissed the phone and hit the off button. "He's having engine problems, but he'll be here as soon as he can get a ride." Kendall paced the room. "In the meantime, you can tell me all about what you did last night."

Lacey patted the couch beside her. "Sit, you're making me nervous."

Kendall dropped onto the couch next to Lacey. "Tell me everything, down to the last dirty detail."

"It was amazing. Just thinking about the two of them makes me so hot I could catch us both on fire."

"The guys must have been really good last night."

Kendall's voice was breathy. She squirmed beside Lacey. "I take it you got off?"

"Several times." Lacey dragged in a deep breath, one hand climbing to her breast, where she tweaked at a nipple through the fabric. "Cory fucked me from behind." Her fingers crossed to the other breast and she pinched and pulled on the taut bud. "I gave Nick a blow job he's not likely to forget for a long time." She wiggled her ass against the couch cushion. "Then Cory held my thighs while Nick fucked me with a beer bottle." Her body tensed as the sensations of the previous night washed over her, her pussy creaming.

"Wow." Kendall crossed her arms over her breasts and ran her tongue across her dry lips. "That sounds wickedly sexy."

Lacey smiled, her eyelids drifting downward. "That was only the half of it."

Kendall breathed hard, her gaze on the door. "What's taking him so long?"

"I'd ask you to share Ed when he gets here, but I wouldn't want to cross the line when you two are so… tight." Lacey sighed, wishing she could still join in the fun of teaching Lacey and Ed how to love each other. But then they had graduated and moved past their need of her coaching skills.

"Go on. Tell me what else Nick did. What about the bottle? I'd never thought about using a bottle to get off on." Kendall pushed her hair back from her forehead and fanned her neck.

Lacey pressed her hand between her legs. "He started by touching me here." She moaned. "It was pure magic, but when he pressed the cool glass bottle against my clit..." Lacey tipped her head back and groaned. "Amaaaazzzing..."

"Holy hell. What happened next?" Kendall unbuttoned the top button of her shirt and ran her hands down the length of her throat. "Damn it's hot in here."

"He slid into me," Lacey said. "Hard and fast."

"Where the hell is Ed?" Kendall wailed.

As if on cue, a knock sounded on the door.

Kendall flew from her seat on the couch and ran for the door.

Male voices sounded in the hallway through the thickness of the wood panel. "I'm sure Lacey's home. Kendall called me a few minutes..."

Kendall yanked open the door and flung herself into Ed Judson's arms. "It's about time you got here." Her legs wrapped around his waist and she clung to him.

Ed's face split into a grin as he stepped across the threshold. "Damn, woman, you'd think I'd been gone a couple weeks, not hours." He kissed her long and hard. When he leaned back, he smiled. "Miss me?"

"Take off your clothes," Kendall demanded.

He chuckled. "I take that as a yes." He stepped to the side and jerked his head to the man standing behind him. "I brought company."

Nick McBride moved into view, his brows dipping as his gaze roamed over Lacey, still sitting on the couch, her hand covering her mons. "Maybe I should go back to work."

Her cheeks burning, Lacey refused to let him know how naughty she felt for being caught talking with another woman about his lovemaking. He didn't have to know he'd been the topic. "Since you hesitated on the ménage last night, it would be a bit of a stretch to think you'd care for a foursome." She winked and forced a casual shrug. "It's up to you. And Ed and Kendall."

Kendall raised her head from slathering Ed's face with kisses to say, "Lacey, you're embarrassing Ed."

"Don't worry about me." Ed laughed, letting Kendall's feet drop to the floor. "I think she's embarrassing Nick more."

Nick's frown deepened. "Are you always so straightforward about sex?"

"I haven't always been." Lacey's lips tightened for a moment, the hurt of her last failed relationship still giving her twinges, like poking at a sensitive scar. "One thing I've learned is that life's too short to beat around the bushes when you can just say what you want."

"I've noticed that about you." Nick shook his head. "You don't pull your punches."

"No, I don't." Lacey nodded. "Leave or stay. Just don't make me waste a good orgasm, for Pete's sake." Lacey stood, the T-shirt slipping downward to cover her nakedness beneath. Let them think what they wanted. She'd sworn never to feel or show shame for wanting—no, needing—sex, ever again. "Well, hell, I'm already losing my edge." She propped her fists on her hips. "Are you going to stand there staring or come in and join the fun?"

"I have to get back to work," Nick said, but he made no move to go.

"Then go." Lacey walked toward the door, throwing

a little more swing into her step than normal. Let him wish he was staying, if in fact he was leaving. For good measure, she leaned past him, brushing her breast against his arm to fling the door open wide. "Don't let us keep you." She turned and flounced away, lifting the edge of her shirt to give him a great view of her naked bottom, before she stopped and flung over her shoulder. "Oh, and close the door behind you, *please*." She emphasized the word *please*, with the same intonation she'd used the night before when she was playing sub to his dom.

Without another look, she joined Kendall as she pulled the buttons loose on Ed's shirt.

"Need a little help there?" Lacey grabbed the garment from behind and peeled it over Ed's broad shoulders.

"Damned female," Nick muttered behind her, and the door slammed shut.

Lacey sagged, disappointed Nick hadn't stayed. "You two want to be alone?"

"Hell, no." Kendall leaned around Ed and grinned. "Ed doesn't mind if you want to watch. Right, Ed? You could even join us..." Her gaze swept past Lacey. "Unless *you* want to do the honors with Lacey?"

Lacey's heart bounced against her ribs.

Before she could turn, hands descended on Lacey's arms. "I'll handle this one." Nick's warm breath fanned across Lacey's shoulder, raising gooseflesh on her arms and sending sparks south to her cooling core, raising the heat level.

"You stayed..." She sighed.

"How could I leave?"

"I thought you wouldn't call or come by? You said—"

"No strings." His fingers tightened painfully, sending another wave of lust straight south. "I meant it."

"But what does a little sex have to do with strings?" Lacey laughed. "Let's get this ball rolling." She spun out of his grip. "I'll be right back. I've been wanting to test out my newest prop."

"Oh, Lacey, you're too much. The woman knows no limits." Kendall laughed as she slipped Ed's zipper down and slid her hand inside his jeans. "Umm, miss me much, big guy?"

In answer, he pulled her top over her head and unclipped her bra, setting her breasts free.

Lacey hurried into her bedroom, afraid if she took too long, Nick would change his mind. And she really didn't want him to change his mind. She wanted to witness his reaction to a little spontaneous orgy.

$\mathcal{N}$ick stood in the middle of the living room, the only one fully clothed and feeling like an idiot, his feet itching to pick up and run. He tried not to watch Ed nibble on Kendall's naked breasts, but he couldn't help it.

"Why *did* you stop by, Nick?" Lacey asked from the shadows of her bedroom.

"Ed dropped his truck off at the shop and needed a ride in an all-fired hurry. And..." he thumbed the silk and lace thong stuffed in the pocket of the gray overalls he'd worn to the shop, his cheeks heating as he scrambled for an answer that wouldn't be too revealing, "...you left something at my apartment last night."

Lacey appeared in her doorway, her beautiful breasts visible through the thin fabric of her shirt, making Nick's cock twitch and harden despite the proximity of the other two people in the room.

"What did I forget?" In her left hand she carried a

riding crop. She tapped it against her thigh and slid it up, catching the edge of her shirt, raising it to display the curly thatch of hair covering her cunt.

Images of what he could do with that crop whipped through Nick's mind, setting his blood on fire. He couldn't leave if he'd wanted to. Walking seemed to be less and less of an option, not with the hard-on forming beneath his coveralls. Holy hell, the woman was making him crazy.

Never in his life had he been in a room with another couple naked and ready to fornicate.

"I know what you're going through." Ed cast a commiserating glance in Nick's direction. "Once these ladies get something in their heads, there's no stopping them."

"That's why you dropped everything and hurried over." Lacey winked at Ed.

The wink made Nick's chest tighten. He wished she'd wink playfully at him.

"Damn right." Ed flicked the tip of Kendall's breast. "I swear Lacey is a witch and can weave spells on men and women alike. I have to look out for my interests." His hand cupped Kendall's breast and he plumped it upward, bending to take it into his mouth. "Woman, you taste like heaven."

Kendall's fingers hooked the tops of Ed's jeans and shoved them over his ass.

Nick shifted a little so that he didn't look like he was staring at his friend's naked butt.

Lacey's mouth turned up in a hint of a teasing smile. "I bet you're uncomfortable around another naked man, aren't you, Nick?" She raised her shirt and ran the riding crop over her belly and up to her breast, tapping lightly. Then she stepped out of the doorway. Instead of crossing to Nick, she aimed for Kendall and Ed. "If you're so dead-set against participating in a ménage, how about watching?" Her brows rose. "Ed? Kendall? Mind if I join you?" Her gaze never left Nick's as she slid behind Ed and helped him toe off his boots. Then she bent to slip his legs out of his jeans, her hands sliding up his calves as she slowly rose. When her fingers reached the curve of his ass, she paused and tipped her head toward Nick. "You know you can join us...if you dare."

Nick's teeth ground together, his fists clenching into tight knots. Oh, he wanted to join them, but in an orgy? He'd never done that before. Now he wondered if he had it in himself to expose his body to two other people he knew as friends. How would their relationship change after making love in a group setting? Would he ever be able to look them in the eye afterward? Did he want to ruin his friendships with Kendall and Ed? "I don't know. It feels strange."

Lacey gave another of her sexy shrugs and cupped Ed's buttocks. "Does that feel strange, Ed?"

"Only if I let it." His hand slid between Kendall's thighs, stroking her pussy. "So far, it feels pretty damned good."

"Are you ashamed that you're turned on by seeing others making love?" Lacey asked, her gaze on Nick, her finger tracing a line between Ed's butt cheeks. "I'll let you use the crop on me if you like. You don't even have to touch Ed." She held out the riding crop, dangling it from her right hand.

Nick almost shot forward, but hesitated.

"Yeah, dude," Ed laughed. "If it's all the same to you, I prefer *women* touching me."

"I didn't say I'd participate," Nick reassured him.

"Offer ends in five, four, three, two—" Lacey's hand started to drop.

Nick shot forward and grabbed the crop. "Okay, but I'm not sold on this. I just stopped by for a minute."

She curled her palm around his cheek. "Honey, sometimes that's all it takes." She grabbed Ed's hips and pressed her pussy against his backside. "Damn, Ed, you make me hot."

"You mean I wasn't doing it for you?" Kendall reached around Ed's waist and tweaked Lacey's nipple. "I'll go down on you, if you like?"

Ed groaned. "You know what that does to me, don't you?"

Kendall grinned at him. "Why do you think I offered?"

"Now you're talking." Lacey moved away and lay on her back in the middle of the throw rug spread out on the living room floor.

Nick's heart hammered against his chest, his cock straining behind his coveralls. He couldn't stop himself from watching, spellbound by the brunette touching her nipples, her belly, her hands sliding low to slip between her folds.

Kendall laughed. "God, Lacey, you're such a tease."

Kendall slipped her jeans off and held her arms open to Ed. "Take me now, or lose me to my girl."

Ed plunged into Kendall, burying his shaft all the way to the hilt.

Kendall threw back her head. "Oh, yes! Sorry, Nick, you're on your own."

"Excuse us while we fuck." Ed walked her into the bedroom and dropped her on the bed, leaving Nick standing in the living room, a riding crop gripped in his hands.

Lacey grinned from the floor, her hand caressing the juncture of her thighs. "I guess it's just you and me. Should you choose to take the challenge."

"Do it, Nick. You know you want it." Kendall called out from the other room, her voice rising with every word until it ended in a squeal. "Ride me, cowboy."

His senses in an uproar, his cock so hard he couldn't breathe, Nick whipped the zipper down and jerked his coveralls off before he could change his mind.

"That's right. Hurry," Lacey urged. Her hips rose, her finger swirling in her juices and twirling over her clit.

Nick toed off his cowboy boots and kicked boots and coveralls aside, standing naked in Lacey's living room while another couple fucked in the bedroom with the door wide open. Surely he'd lost his mind, but he didn't give a damn.

Lacey reached out. "Over here. Straddle my head and come closer."

He knelt on the floor, a knee on each side of her head, dropped to his palms, his face hovering over

Lacey's cunt. "I'll take over from here." He brushed her hands aside and lowered himself over her.

"Faster, Ed. I'm so close," Kendall moaned from the other room.

"Shouldn't we let the others catch up with us?" Ed muttered. "I feel so selfish."

"You're kidding, right?" Kendall gasped. "Lacey can get there with a vibrator and her imagination. She doesn't need us." A smacking sound was followed by Kendall's demand, "Give it to me."

So hot his dick throbbed, Nick threaded his fingers through Lacey's curls, parting her folds to expose her swollen clit. He bent to taste her, amazed at how willing she was to make love with others present. Perhaps it had to do with her insistence on no strings attached. With others around, she couldn't establish that certain level of intimacy a blossoming relationship required.

Fine by him. After the slew his ex had dragged him through, he wasn't in any hurry to jump back into matrimonial mayhem.

Cool fingers curled around his cock, tugging gently.

She took him into her mouth, sliding her tongue around his length as he pushed deeper. One hand wrapped around his balls and massaged them between her fingers. The other hand clutched his ass, pulling him down, down, down, until his dick bumped the back of her throat. Warm, wet, and tongued, he couldn't think of anything better unless it was sliding into her pussy, burying himself all the way to the hilt.

He lapped at her juices, tracing her entrance with the tip of his tongue. Then he flicked her clit, tapping at that special place that had her screaming out, loud enough for the neighbors to hear.

Her back arched, her hips rising, offering more for his taking.

Nick didn't let up, relentless in his determination to make her crazy with lust, the way she'd made him. Ever since he'd woken that morning, his cock as hard as the night before, he hadn't been able to stop thinking about her. Cramming her panties in his pocket had been a very bad idea. Every time he'd stuffed his hand in there and felt the silk and lace, he had an instantaneous hard-on, making it nearly impossible to work through the backlog of auto repairs he had waiting for him to complete.

When Ed had shown up with his truck needing repairs, Nick was glad for the company and a chance to get Lacey off his mind. Kendall's call resulting in Ed's sudden need to get to Kendall and Lacey left Nick volunteering to take Ed to Lacey's apartment.

Nick had rationalized to himself that it was an opportunity to return the panties burning a hole in his pocket. He'd drop off Ed and the panties and go right back to work. When Ed got in Nick's truck and let it slip that he was on his way to join Kendall and Lacey having a little girl sex, Nick's curiosity and penis got the better of him.

Nick hadn't been able to climb the stairs fast enough, following Ed up to Lacey's apartment. He'd made the mistake of peering over Ed's shoulder at a nearly naked Lacey.

After that, he couldn't have left if the house had gone

up in flames. He'd have stayed and seen this through, despite his pathetic attempt at a protest.

Now, with Lacey's clit sucked into his mouth and her lips wrapped around his dick, he couldn't think past the rush of adrenaline and sensations spurring him on. He jack-hammered in and out of Lacey's mouth, while nibbling and tickling her into a frenzy he prayed she couldn't deny.

As the moment intensified, he sensed Lacey tensing beneath him. Her hands moved across his ass in jerky, clawing strokes. Her heels pressed against the floor, raising her hips up. She backed off his cock. "More, oh dear angels in heaven, more."

He gave it to her, drawing her body tighter and tighter until her bowstring of control snapped and she grew rigid, her fingernails driving into his buttocks.

As she rocked with each spasm and shook with the force of her orgasm, Nick rose, grabbed the riding crop and flipped her onto her stomach, raising her ass into the air. He slapped the crop against a soft, rounded cheek. "Like that?" he asked.

"Oh, yes," she said. "More!"

He popped her again, this time leaving a red line against the pale white skin. "Damn. Did that hurt?"

"Yes...no...oh God, I need you inside me," she said, her cheek pressed to the rug, her bottom high, her pussy dripping.

"Hang on." He fumbled for his jeans pocket, ripping his wallet out and rifling through until he unearthed a condom. With deft movements, he ripped it out of the packet and rolled it down over his straining member, all the while gritting his teeth to keep from coming too soon. When he was ready, Nick popped her with the riding crop once more. When she hissed, he grabbed her hips and thrust into her, driving all the way until his balls banged against her.

"Harder." Her fingers dug into the carpet. "Faster."

"Okay, Ed," Kendall said from the other room. "That's your cue to turn up the heat."

Bedsprings squeaked, matching the pace of Nick's thrusts.

Having another couple fucking in the apartment at the same time should have been distracting to Nick. Instead, it set his senses ablaze, pushing him to slam into Lacey so hard their naked bodies made slapping sounds as they banged together.

"My hair. Pull it," Lacey urged.

Beyond rational thought, past mere passion to explosive, uncontrolled lust, he grabbed a hank of her hair and pulled back hard, at the same time whipping her thigh with the crop.

She cried out, "Yes!"

Nick rode her like the wild creature she was, fucking, pulling, whipping until he launched over the precipice, bursting through the heavens with an orgasm so cataclysmic he dropped the whip, let go of her hair and grasped her hips to hold her steady, to ease the intensity and friction so that he could savor the moment, catch his breath and absorb a pleasure so intense it was painful. His cock throbbed, his heart raced and he had the sudden urge to pound his chest and roar.

Slowly, as he returned to earth, he eased Lacey to her belly, lying down on top of her, his legs shaking and his mind a raw blur. "What the hell just happened?" he whispered into her ear.

"Nick, my man, you just had the best sex of your entire life." Ed emerged from the bedroom dragging his jeans up over his hips. "Lacey, you should be ashamed of taking advantage of him like that."

She lay with her face pressed to the rug, her body limp.

Nick rolled off her and smoothed a hand over her back, for the first time noticing the red welts he'd left with the riding crop. "Lacey? Are you okay?"

"No."

Guilt sank deep in his gut like a two-ton weight. "Did I hurt you?"

"No. Yes," she murmured. "I think I'm going to die."

"Where does it hurt? Should I call an ambulance?" Nick stared at her lying on her belly, afraid to move her, afraid of hurting her more.

"No. Don't do that." She rolled onto her back, her arm falling over her face. She drew in a long, shaky breath and let it out. When her arm dropped to her side, she smiled up at him. "Damn, Nick. That was good."

He let out the breath he'd held. "You bring out the animal in me."

"Yeah." She grinned. "It's a gift." Lacey held out her hand. "Help me up, will ya?"

He rose to his feet and gripped her hand, pulling her up against him, his arm circling her waist. "Now what?"

Her brows rose. "I don't know about you, but I have

a hair appointment and if I'm not mistaken, you have to go back to work."

"Will I see you tonight?" he asked.

"Only if you're planning on going to the Ugly Stick. I'll be working." She pulled away from Nick and slipped an arm around Kendall. "Thanks for stopping by." She leaned up on tip-toe and kissed Ed's cheek, then laid a kiss on Kendall's lips. "Always a pleasure to see you two. Don't be strangers, just because you moved out."

Kendall grabbed her clothes and handed Ed's shirt to him. "I'll give you a ride home."

Ed dragged his shirt over his shoulders and pinched Kendall's ass as she stepped into her jeans. "We can go for round two when we get there. I should be up for it by then."

She slapped at his arm. "You're insatiable."

He grabbed her and hauled her naked breasts against his bare chest. "Only because of you, sweetheart."

A pang of envy thumped inside Nick's chest. Watching Ed and Kendall play with each other reminded him of how a relationship should be, what he'd thought he'd had when he'd first married. But all that had changed as soon as he'd said *I do*.

"Here." Lacey handed him his coveralls and boots. "I'd see you to the door, but I'm headed for the shower. Thanks for a good time." She turned away without so much as squeezing his arm or giving him a kiss.

"That's it?" he asked before he could stop himself.

Lacey faced him, her brows raised. "What do you mean?"

"We just made love."

She tipped her head. "Yes, and?"

And what? He didn't know what to say to that, he knew leaving like he was just wasn't right. There should be more to it than being shown the door. Hell, she wasn't even showing him the door.

He shook his head. "Never mind." Without saying another word, he stalked out the door to Lacey's apartment and slammed the door behind him. He dropped his boots on the landing, slipped into his coveralls and boots and stomped out to his truck, reminding himself he'd been adamant about no strings, and Lacey had been equally vocal on the "no attachment" issue.

Why that bothered him now was beyond him. He should be happy that Lacey didn't want a commitment out of him. He sure as hell wasn't ready for one, nor would he ever be after his first wife's betrayal.

He climbed in behind the wheel of his pickup, shoved the gearshift into reverse and whipped out onto the road, burning a layer of rubber off a perfectly good set of tires.

Everything was well on its way to being right in his world. Footloose, fancy-free and divorced. What more could he ask for?

Damned if he knew why he was so pissed off.

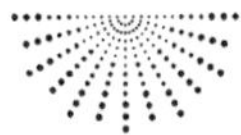

"What's with the huge grin?" Audrey cornered Lacey in the storeroom later that evening.

Lacey reached for a case of whiskey, avoiding Audrey's direct gaze. "I don't know what you're talking about." Her lips quirked as an image of Nick flashed through her mind.

"That." Audrey jumped in front of her, blocking her path to the whiskey. "Last night you were so down in the mouth I thought you were going to slit your wrists. Tonight, you've been smiling like the cat that ate the canary. Not that I'm complaining. At least you're not scaring the customers." She propped a fist on her hip. "What gives?"

"Nothing." Lacey's grin widened. "Oh, hell, I can't keep anything from you. I had the best sex ever last night and today."

Audrey squealed and shoved Lacey backward until

she was forced to sit on a stack of boxes. "You're not getting out of here until you tell me all the details. Don't leave any of them out." She crossed her arms. "Who with?"

"Cory…" Lacey ticked off on her finger.

"Our Cory who dances on Ladies' Night? Is he even old enough to have sex?" Audrey answered for herself. "Oh, yeah, he couldn't dance at the bar if he wasn't at least twenty-one." Her gaze pinned Lacey's. "Damn, woman, you scored with Cory? I'm impressed."

Lacey frowned. "I'm not much older than he is. Geez, you make it sound like I'm robbing the cradle."

"Not at all. I'm envious. If I wasn't getting some with Jackson…"

"You wouldn't go for Cory, he works for you." Lacey raised a second finger. "Then there was Cory's big brother." Her face softened, a rush of heat filling her core, moistening her channel. "Nick."

"Nick the mechanic?" Audrey pulled her tank top out, flapping it. "He's hot. Wow, I'm even more impressed. Last night and today?"

"No, the two of them were last night. Today, Kendall showed up at my apartment and we had a little fun…" Lacey shrugged, "…once Ed showed up."

"You, Ed and Kendall?" Audrey fanned herself. "You're making me hot just thinking about it."

"Ed wasn't alone." Lacey stood and made to step around Audrey. "Nick was with him. That's when it got hot."

"I'm surprised you're able to walk." Audrey's smile flipped. "What happened to no commitment?"

"Ed and Kendall know I'm no threat to their relationship. And I made it clear to Nick and Cory, no strings. Nick was all for it and Cory was just in it for the fun."

"Are you sure?"

"Oh, yeah." Lacey had sensed Nick's reluctance where relationships and commitment were concerned. She wondered what had happened to turn him against love and happily ever after. Had he had a bad marriage like she had?

"Two times with the sexy mechanic in two days…" Audrey shook her head. "Sounds like more than just casual sex to me."

"*Convenient* sex. Don't read more into it than that." Lacey couldn't move past Audrey without tripping over her. "I bet the customers are yowling for their drinks by now. I should get back to work."

"Be careful, Lacey." Audrey caught her arm. "I'd hate to see you hurt again."

"It's just sex."

"The more you see Nick, the harder it will be to walk away."

"Not this time." Lacey pulled free of Audrey's grip and stepped around her. "I won't make the same mistake twice. He's just another pretty face and great body. That's all."

"Ever considered that not all men are as stupid and duplicitous as your ex?"

"That might be true, but I don't plan on letting one close enough to test the theory."

"You could be missing the love of your life, your perfect match, like I found in Jackson."

The dreamy look in Audrey's eyes made Lacey want to gag. "I'm not worried. The perfect match for me doesn't exist." Lacey left the storeroom with a knot in her gut and feeling the urge to run as far and fast as she could.

Unfortunately, there was a barroom full of thirsty cowboys and she couldn't leave Audrey in the lurch. Not after all her boss had done for her. So she squared her shoulders and threw herself into the work of waiting tables, flipping bottles and putting on a sassy show for the patrons of the Ugly Stick.

If her gaze strayed toward the entrance a little too often, she chalked it up to sizing up the crowd for future drink orders. She refused to admit she was looking for Nick to step through the door.

After ten o'clock rolled around, she'd given up on Nick. A busy mechanic with a business to run and early morning hours didn't go out drinking every night of the week.

A stab of disappointment hit Lacey low in the belly.

I won't call so don't wait by the phone. I'm not interested in a relationship. Nick's words echoed in Lacey's head. Exactly her sentiments before they'd started.

Now…

"Thinking about me, beautiful?" Warm hands slipped around her waist and pulled her against a wall of hard muscle.

Lacey's body flushed with the heated memories the voice inspired and she turned with a smile on her

face, happier than she should have been. "N—
Oh, Cory."

She tried, but couldn't keep the smile. It faded with
her fleeting burst of happy anticipation.

Cory laughed. "If I was a bettin' man, I'd bet you
were hoping for Nick." He hugged her. "Sorry, but he
didn't ride with me. He was still working at the garage
when I dropped off his dinner an hour ago."

"Don't be silly," Lacey lied. "I'm very happy to see
you." She hooked his elbow with hers and led him to a
stool at the bar. "Let me buy you a drink."

"I haven't stopped thinking about you after
last night."

"Oh, really?" She'd stopped thinking about Cory as
soon as she'd left their apartment early that morning.
Nick had been the one to keep her awake into the wee
hours. She turned away from the younger McBride.
Don't go there, Lacey. Remember, no obsessing over a man.

Before she could step behind the safety of the bar,
Cory grabbed her hand. "Did you say something?"

"No, I didn't." Her cheeks heated with her second lie
of the night. Lacey tugged her arm free of Cory's grip
and slipped behind the bar, keeping her face lowered so
telltale signs of her lie weren't obvious. "What will
you have?"

"A shot of whiskey, make it a double." Cory's voice
sounded deeper, more like his brother Nick's.

Her hand on the bottle of whiskey, Lacey frowned.
"Isn't that a bit strong for a college—" She glanced up,
into Nick McBride's dark gaze. The whiskey bottle
slipped from her fingers.

As soon as it left her hand, Lacey dove to catch it, a graceless save that cost her a broken fingernail and a mini heart attack. "Oh, hi, Nick. When did you get here?"

"Just did." He'd changed out of the coverall he'd worn earlier that day when he'd stopped by her apartment. Jeans, neatly pressed chambray shirt and cowboy boots made him look almost sexier than when he'd stood naked in front of her. Hell, she'd had a thing for hot cowboys ever since she'd gone to work for Audrey at the Ugly Stick. And this one was *caliente*!

Lacey's heart hammered against her ribs. "Well, that's nice." Her hand shook as she poured a double shot of whiskey and slid it across the counter toward Nick.

When he reached for it, their fingers touched and something like a spark of electricity ignited between them.

Lacey flinched, her gaze shooting up to capture Nick's. Had he felt it too?

His dark brows drew together, forming a deep V. "Thank you." He lifted the glass and downed it in one swallow.

"Want another?"

"No, I have to drive home."

"If you'll excuse me, I see Mona," Cory said. "I wanted to ask her about the plans for the Sadie Hawkins dance and fundraiser. I promised I'd put together a kissing booth with some of my buddies from college."

Lacey heard Cory's words, but she couldn't take her

eyes off Nick. "That should make a pile of money. What charity will the money go to?"

"Temptations safe house for homeless clowns." Cory grinned.

Lacey blinked and shook her head and turned to Cory. "Homeless clowns? What are you talking about?"

"Got your attention, didn't I?" The younger McBride grinned. "It's for the children's hospital." He slapped his brother's back. "See ya later, bro."

Nick muttered, "Right. Later." Then as if surfacing from a trance, he shot a look in his brother's direction. "Let me know if you need a designated driver to get you home tonight."

"I'm not drinking." Cory patted his flat stomach. "Gotta keep up my girlish figure for the kissing booth." He winked at Lacey. "Maybe we'll see you tonight after work?"

Images of Lacey naked and Cory fucking her from behind flashed through Nick's head. He glared at Cory. "I'm sure she'll be exhausted by then."

Lacey's brows rose. "I tend to be a night owl. But I'll bet Nick has an early morning at the shop, so I won't trouble you two. I'll leave my door unlocked if you want to come up and talk or…whatever."

Cory shrugged. "I might take you up on that. That way old Nick can get some sleep."

Nick fought back a growl. "Don't you have classes tomorrow?"

Cory grinned. "Not until noon. See ya later, Lacey." He waved and took off toward Mona.

"I don't know how he keeps up his grades staying up all hours," Nick muttered.

Lacey's gaze followed Cory, a smile curling her lips.

Nick's chest tightened. He didn't own Lacey. He had no say over her influence on his little brother. But damn it, she was older and more experienced. What if Cory fancied himself in love with the gorgeous brunette? She'd already told them she wasn't interested in a long-term relationship. Cory was young enough to still believe love conquered all. "He's going to make a good doctor some day," Nick blurted.

Her brown-eyed gaze swung toward him and away from Cory. "Yes, I believe he will."

"He has another four or more years of school after he finishes his undergrad degree."

"That's a big commitment."

"Yeah, I hope he stays the course." Nick's gaze captured hers. "I wouldn't want anything to distract him from his studies."

Lacey planted her fists on her hips. "Are you warning me away from your little brother?"

Nick's cheeks heated. "No, of course not, I'm just…"

"You don't want me to hit on Cory, do you?"

"He's got a lot of school… He needs his sleep…he's got to focus." Oh hell. Nick realized he should have kept his mouth shut. Now he'd dug a hole the size of Texas and he couldn't get out of it without some help.

"Nick, honey, so glad to see you. It's been a while."

Audrey draped an arm over his shoulders and smiled. "That garage of yours keeping you busy?"

"Yes, ma'am." Nick turned away from Lacey's glare.

"I heard about your divorce." She hugged him. "Nasty bit of business having to sell your spread and split the proceeds."

"I'm doin' all right." His fist closed around the empty shot glass. "Still have the shop."

"I hear you're workin' it." Audrey clapped a hand to his back. "Care to take this ol' girl around the dance floor one time?"

"I don't know. I tend to be all left feet."

"I'll take my chances."

Trish hadn't wanted to go out dancing since the day they'd gotten married. With him, anyway. From what he'd learned through the grapevine, she'd been cuttin' a rug in the neighboring county. If he'd known it during the divorce, and that she'd been having an affair, he would have stuck to his guns and kept the ranch. She'd led him to believe it was his fault their marriage didn't last. He'd given her everything her lawyer demanded, guilt playing a big part of the concessions. He'd even begged her to stay and give their marriage another chance. Not so much because he loved her, but because he hated admitting failure at anything.

Now that the divorce was final and all the dirty laundry had been discovered, he wished he'd taken more time to investigate and ferret out the truth.

Audrey hooked his arm and tugged him out of the chair. "Come on, I think you need this more than I do."

Nick dared a glance at Lacey.

Her eyes shot daggers at him and he knew he deserved them. "Yeah, I think I do."

Once out on the floor, and under Audrey's lead, Nick got his dancin' legs under him and settled into a smooth Texas Two-Step. "Thanks, Audrey."

"I shouldn't speak out of turn, but Lacey is kinda in the same boat as you."

"How so?"

"Her ex cheated on her and left her high and dry. She's dead set on never getting hitched again, and who would blame her?"

So Lacey had been dumped as well. "That explains a lot."

"Yeah, a lot of us have been down the wrong path a time or two. It takes the right person to make us want to try a new one."

Nick glanced at Lacey, weaving through the tables, balancing a tray full of beer mugs and long-necks. "I'm not in the market for a wife."

"You may not be, but sometimes the best thing to ever happen to you happens when you least want or expect it. Don't let it slip through your hands because some stupid woman hurt your pride."

"I loved Trish," Nick argued.

"Yeah, and that's why she filed for divorce based on neglect." Audrey patted his arm. "If you'd really loved her, you would have had a hard time leaving her alone." Audrey spun away from him as the music came to a halt. "Thanks for the dance."

Left standing on the dance floor, his head spinning from what Audrey had said, Nick glanced around at the tables, hoping to find someone he could sit with so that he didn't have to talk to Lacey. There was an empty seat at the table with Mark and Luke Gray Wolf.

As he crossed the floor toward them, Libby Jones stepped between them, setting a bottle of beer in front of each. When she turned to leave, Mark grabbed her around the middle and pulled her into his lap. She squealed and laughed, planting a kiss on his lips. When he set her back on her feet, Luke didn't let her get far before he tugged her into his lap and kissed her soundly.

No. Nick didn't feel like being around all that hugging, laughing and kissing. It reminded him too much of what he'd always thought love would be. Fun. Sexy. Absolute commitment by both parties in the union. In Mark, Luke and Libby's case, make that *all* parties in the union. How the brothers could share her was a mystery to Nick. Perhaps because they were so close in age and were twins, they were used to sharing everything—even their woman.

Ed sat at the bar, stealing every bit of Kendall's spare minutes between the time she took orders and delivered them to the tables.

Finally Nick allowed himself to look for Lacey, though he'd been tracking her in his peripheral vision all along. She was in the farthest corner of the bar.

Nick opted for the empty stool next to Ed, praying the man didn't mention their afternoon sex session with Kendall and Lacey.

"Can I buy you a beer?" Ed asked.

"Thanks." Nick eased onto the stool and propped his boots on the brass footrail ringing the bar.

Libby returned to the bar, her face flushed and her tank top twisted. "What can I get you boys?"

Ed paid for Nick's beer and the two men twisted on their stools to look out over the crowd, each nursing a frothy mug, dripping with condensation.

"Can't get over how lucky I am." Ed shook his head.

"How so?"

"Kendall."

Well damn. As soon as he mentioned Kendall, the image of Kendall and Lacey naked in Lacey's apartment popped into Nick's mind. "Yeah, you're lucky, all right."

"Hey, now, don't go getting any ideas about her. I've staked my claim and she's agreed. We're getting married next spring."

Nick held up his hands. "I never said I wanted her." His gaze slipped across the room to Lacey.

"No, you haven't. And you handled the situation well at lunch today."

"Just tell me to shut the fuck up if I'm being nosy, but is Lacey a permanent part of your relationship with Kendall?"

"Lacey?" Ed laughed. "I think she likes to shock people. Her ex was a prick and apparently unimaginative when it came to sex. I think Lacey's making up for lost time."

"Kendall doesn't mind sharing you with Lacey?"

"Lacey helped me open my eyes about Kendall. I owe her a lot and besides that, she adds a lot of spice to our sex life." He grinned. "I guess I don't have to tell *you* that."

Just the idea of discussing sex with the man who had been fornicating with his fiancée in the same apartment as Nick when he was having his way with Lacey had Nick all hot and bothered. He shifted on the stool and loosened the top button of his shirt. "How are you managing the ranch in this heat?"

Ed laughed. "Got a creek on the ranch. Kendall and I go skinny-dipping a lot."

Nick was thankful the music started up again, conveniently covering his groan. He still hadn't fixed the AC in their apartment and it promised to be another hot night. Even hotter knowing Lacey would be upstairs, probably sleeping naked. Damn the woman for starting something when Nick had been perfectly content to remain celibate. He downed the last swig of beer and slammed the bottle on the counter, his gaze going back to the barroom, picking up on the woman who'd made his life a new kind of hell.

"Hey, big guy, you're scaring the patrons." Kendall tapped Nick's shoulder, wedged herself between the two men and set her tray of empty mugs and bottles on the counter. She gave her order to Libby, the bartender, and let Ed pull her onto his lap. "Umm, that's nice. My feet are killing me."

"I'll rub them for you when you get home tonight."

"I hope you'll rub more than that." She wiggled her bottom over his crotch, then hopped up when Libby completed her order. "I'll be counting the minutes."

After Kendall darted off between the tables, Nick stood. "Thanks for the beer."

"Thanks for sticking around at lunch. Lacey's a lot of woman for just one man and Kendall more than satisfies any itch I might have."

"Don't mention it." Nick frowned. "Really, don't mention it. I'm not sure what happened."

"That's the beauty of life with Lacey. She likes doing the unpredictable. I kinda miss living in the building with her." Ed stood and clapped a hand across Nick's back. "But then you'll get used to it. If she fancies you as much as I think she does, you're in for a helluva ride."

Nick glanced once more at Lacey and left the bar, determined to go back to the apartment and bed. He had a lot of work at the shop and until his house was finished, he'd be better off steering clear of the woman in the apartment upstairs.

LACEY BREATHED a sigh of relief when Nick left the bar. Now she could focus on her work, maybe even flirt with a few cowboys to get her mind off Nick. He'd been hot naked, hot in his coveralls and even hotter in his jeans and cowboy boots. How the hell was she supposed to get him out of her head when he kept popping up? She'd already spilled two drinks, dropped a bottle when she'd been flipping it and tripped over a pair of men's size-twelve boots. By the time midnight rolled around, Audrey cornered her and told her to go home before she put her out of business. She did it in a nice way, but it still hit home that Lacey had let a man get under her skin.

As she pulled up to the apartment house, she noted that the light was on in the living room of the downstairs apartment. Cory's invitation echoed in her head. At least one of the McBrides wanted her to stop in. Lacey had half a mind to do just that and to hell with Nick's warning to leave Cory alone.

As she entered the building, her feet slowed in front of their door and her hand rose to knock.

At the last second, she changed her mind. If he wanted to see her, he'd have to come to her this time. And she wasn't so sure she wanted him to.

Halfway up the stairs, she realized what she'd been thinking and which *he* she'd been thinking about. Damn. She was doing exactly what she'd promised herself she'd never do again. She was obsessing over a man.

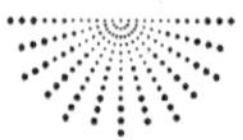

Nick stood on the other side of the apartment door. Though he'd sat in the recliner pretending to read a book, he couldn't deny he'd been waiting for the sound of Lacey's car pulling into the drive.

"You can relax, she's home." Cory emerged from his bedroom, smiling.

"She who?"

"Come on. You told me yourself that you normally hit the sack before midnight." Cory glanced at the clock on the wall. "It's one in the morning and you get up at seven. Why else would you be awake?"

"I was reading." Nick nodded toward the book lying open on the end table, his ears cocked for the sound of Lacey's car door slamming shut.

"You have to be the slowest reader ever." Cory crossed to the book and lifted it. "You've been on the same page for the past hour."

Busted.

Nick shrugged. "I have a lot on my mind."

"Lacey is a lot of woman."

"I'm not interested in her."

"Then why did you show up at the Ugly Stick for the second weeknight in a row? You've been an old man since the day you graduated college—going to bed at a decent hour, only going out on weekends, and living the life of a saint. No wonder you're conflicted. Lacey's got your boxers in a knot, hasn't she?"

"No, that's not it at all. The contractor is dragging his feet on the house, and I hate imposing on you."

"Uh-huh." Cory moved the curtain aside. "She's on her way up the steps. I wonder if she'll take me up on stopping by." Cory crossed the room to the front door.

Nick frowned. "That's crazy. She was here last night." They'd had hot sex at lunch that day. His cock twitched at the memory. Why would she stop by for more?

Cory's hand reached for the doorknob. "Should I ask her in?"

Nick headed him off, leaping for the door. "No."

Cory chuckled. "Afraid of the woman?"

"Don't you have some studying to do?" Nick glared, standing between Cory and the door, his arms crossed.

"As a matter of fact, I do." Cory winked. "Maybe your problem is that you don't like to share. There-fore...I'll leave you two alone."

"She's not coming in."

"I'll let you handle that one."

Cory entered his room and closed the door behind him.

Footsteps sounded on the wood flooring in the hallway outside the apartment door.

Nick reached for the doorknob, his hand curling around it, his hearing picking up on the slowed footfalls.

He could sense her on the other side of the wood paneling. Nick's heart raced, his palms sweated and he could almost feel the soft touch of her skin against his, smell the fragrant herbal scent of her hair. He closed his eyes and waited for the soft knock. Behind his zipper, his dick swelled in eager anticipation of another encounter with Lacey.

After several seconds, the knock didn't come and footsteps moved away from the door, fading up the staircase leading to Lacey's apartment.

Nick opened his eyes and stared at the door. "What the hell?"

"Ha! She didn't take me up on my offer." Cory stood in his open doorway. "Maybe she's not in the mood. Or maybe she's not in the mood for *me*." He shrugged. "I got the feeling she was more interested in you to begin with. It won't hurt my feelings if you follow her up the stairs."

Nick frowned. "I'm not chasing after any woman."

"Give her a kiss for me, will ya?" Cory's laughter echoed through the living room as he closed the door to his room again.

Nick paced the length of the living room and back to the front door. "This is insane," he muttered.

"Lacey has been known to make men crazy," Cory called out through the paneling.

"What are the doors around here made of, fuckin' paper?" Nick groused.

"Yes. Didn't I tell you?"

Hell no, Cory hadn't mentioned that fact.

Dragging in a deep breath, Nick held it then let it out. Why wasn't he asleep? He had three cars on the racks at the shop that needed fixin' tomorrow. Hell, today. If he didn't get some sleep, he'd be no good to anyone.

Nick made an about-face and headed for his bedroom. He had just ended a bad marriage, he sure as hell didn't need another woman lousing up his life.

He stripped out of his clothes and lay down naked on the sheets, the heat making it difficult to get comfortable. The thought that he might be lying beneath Lacey's bedroom and she might be naked as well, made Nick's cock swell all the more.

Damn.

As soon as he closed his eyes, images of Lacey with her ass in the air and him pulling her hair with one hand while whipping her with the crop had him groaning.

This was never going to work. He sat up, jammed his legs into his jeans and carefully tucked his erection beneath the denim. Shirtless, he exited the apartment, walked outside, barefoot, onto the front porch and sat on the steps. The night air was a little cooler than the stuffy air in the apartment. He had to get the AC fixed before another day went by or he'd never get any sleep.

"Can't sleep either?" a silken voice called out from the other end of the porch.

Nick spun to glance up at Lacey sitting on the porch swing, dressed in a filmy, sheer nightgown, her hair falling softly around her shoulders, the light from his living room shining through the open window, gilding her brown hair with a golden glow.

"Too hot." Nick realized his comment had nothing to do with the air temperature and everything to do with Lacey.

"My AC works if you'd like to come up."

His cock jerked beneath his fly and he stretched his legs out in front of him to ease the discomfort. "No, thanks."

She chuckled. "Afraid I might demand sex in trade for a cool place to sleep?"

He didn't answer. If he was smart, he'd walk away, but he couldn't, and he couldn't look away. "I'm not in the market for a relationship."

She tipped her head, one foot tucked beneath her, the other tapping the porch decking, setting the swing in motion. "I thought we'd established that up front." Her eyes widened. "Did you think I wanted more?" Lacey shook her head, her hair brushing against her shoulders. "I've been burned before. I have no desire to do it again."

Nick's focus remained on the long, slender leg flexing and bending as the swing rocked back and forth. The silence lengthened between them. Finally, Nick said, "Me too."

"I take it you're still a little raw from the experience."

He shrugged.

Another long silence.

"Have you always been a grease monkey?" Lacey asked.

Nick's lips twisted. "Have you always been a waitress?"

She smiled, the simple act making her look years younger, almost a teenager. "No. I got my accounting degree, but never took my CPA exam."

Nick stared at Lacey, shaking his head. "Sorry, I just can't see you as a mild-mannered accountant."

"That makes us even. I can't see you as having always been a mechanic."

"I wasn't." He stood. "Look, I'm sorry about warning you off Cory. You and he have a right to do whatever you want. I have a hard time remembering he isn't a kid anymore."

"You're forgiven." Lacey lips twitched. "For the record, I have no intention of leading Cory on."

Nick turned to stare out at the night, feeling more relaxed, the silence lengthening between them again. A comfortable silence. He glanced back at Lacey where she sat on the swing, wanting to go to her and wrap his arms around her. "Wanna go for a walk?"

She glanced down at her skimpy outfit. "Like this?"

"You might want to put something less revealing on in case the Temptation cops are on patrol."

"Shouldn't you be going to bed?"

Oh, that was where he wanted to go all right, but not to sleep, and he wanted to avoid having sex with Lacey, if for no other reason than to prove to himself that he was capable of resisting her feminine allure. "I can't sleep, and I need to burn off some energy. Are you coming?"

She hopped up, leaving the swing swaying in the breeze. "I'll only be a minute."

LACEY RACED UP THE STAIRS, her feet barely making a sound as she climbed to the top landing and entered her open door. In less than a minute, she'd whipped off the nightgown and slipped into a pair of shorts, a tank top and her cowboy boots.

Her body ached for release from the sexual tension she'd been knotted up with since she'd seen Nick earlier in the bar. If she wasn't going to have sex with him, a walk might help. Then maybe she could go to bed alone and not resort to her vibrator.

The trip down the stairs was noisier than going up, her boot heels clicking on the wooden risers.

Nick stepped out of his apartment, wearing his boots and a T-shirt over his jeans.

Lacey stared at the way his T-shirt clung to his muscular chest, thinking it was a shame to cover it.

"Just for the record, I liked the other outfit better." Nick didn't wait for her response. He stepped out onto the porch and held the door open.

Her cheeks warming, Lacey smiled. "I liked your earlier outfit better too," she murmured as she slipped by him, resisting the urge to touch a hand to his chest and feel the solid muscles hidden beneath the jersey knit.

Nick walked beside her along the sidewalk, his expression hidden in the shadows.

If she couldn't read his face, he couldn't read hers. Something about the anonymity of the darkness made her feel more relaxed, more open to a candid conversation, less inhibited.

"I can't get over how hot it's been these last few days." Lacey tugged at her tank, pulling the fabric away from her skin. The movement of air over her breasts made them pucker, the tips turning into tight little beads. Or was it the hot cowboy-mechanic walking beside her?

Either way, the snack at lunch wasn't nearly enough to satisfy her, now that she knew what Nick had to offer. But he seemed determined to keep her at arm's length for the duration of their walk.

Lacey would play along...for a little while. "Why haven't I noticed you before?"

His shoulders rose and lowered. "I haven't been hanging out at the Ugly Stick much."

"Not your thing?"

"Not my wife's thing," he admitted.

Her feet slamming to a halt, Lacey stood still, her heart thumping against her rib cage. "Your wife?" Shit. She'd thought he was divorced. Had she been screwing another woman's man?

Nick stopped a couple steps ahead of her and turned back, his lips twisted. "Ex-wife."

"Oh. Well, then..." Lacey's pulse returned to normal and she caught up with Nick.

The man beside her chuckled. "I thought you didn't have any boundaries."

"I don't. At least not many. I do have one though, and that is that I don't poach on another woman's man, unless they're both willing. I'm not a home-wrecker." She scuffed her boot on a pebble, sending it flying across the pavement.

"Me either." Nick caught up with the rock she'd kicked and tapped it with the tip of his cowboy boot. "I get the feeling there's a story to go with that anger."

She snorted. "It would bore you."

"Try me."

"I have and there's a lot to like." Her gaze slid over him from head to foot. Even in the shadows, his silhouette inspired a flush of heat to wash over her.

"No, really, what happened?"

"I was young and naive. He was having an affair and I couldn't see it until the ladies of the Temptation Garden Club pointed it out to me." The remembered humiliation of that day chilled her desire. She wrapped her arms around herself, her shoulders stiffening, her fists clenching.

"Wow. And I thought it was bad enough finding out that my wife was fucking the gardener."

Lacey laid a hand on his arm. "Tell me the bitch wasn't doing it in your bed."

He nodded. "Call me a fool. I took the vows seriously."

"And she didn't." Lacey squeezed his arm. "I'm sorry."

"Why? Our breakup was a good thing. We weren't

meant to be together. I was too infatuated to realize that."

"How so?" She slipped her arm through his, hooking his elbow.

"She wanted the posh life surrounded by servants and people." He sighed. "I wanted a simple life on a ranch with animals that I cared for, out away from everything. Maybe a kid or two."

"Sounds lovely."

"Which one?" Nick leaned away from her, staring down at her. "Her idea of how things should be or mine?"

"Yours." Lacey stared out into the darkness, visualizing her own dreams of a house in the country with a wide front porch lined with rockers. And children playing in the yard. "Guess it takes a fool to know a fool."

"Right." Nick resumed walking.

Lacey's steps matched his as they entered the area of town with the older, larger homes. "Now what?"

"What do you mean?"

"What are your plans? Are you giving up on your dreams of that ranch and the animals?"

"Not really. I had to sell the house and land I owned as part of the divorce settlement."

"That bitch."

He shrugged. "It wasn't a big spread and I couldn't go back in the house. Not after…"

"After your bed had been violated." Lacey's heart squeezed tight when his head nodded. "Man, that was low. At least my ex had the decency to do it in the office or a hotel. As far as I know, he never did it with her in my bed."

"The man must have been an ass."

"So we made mistakes."

"I guess that's why you're adamant about not committing to anyone."

"I, for one, don't plan on making the same mistake twice."

"Me either," Nick said softly.

"Thanks for telling me. I know how hard it is."

"Same."

Lacey paused outside the front of a large Victorian home. "You know who lives here?"

Nick shook his head.

Lacey grabbed his hand. "Judge Stephens. Come on." She dragged him toward the side of the house.

"Where are we going?"

"He's got a pool in the backyard." She shot a look up at him, her heartbeat skipping along. "I'm hot and you said you were too."

"So?"

"We're going swimming." As soon as she pushed him through the hedges surrounding the backyard, she dropped his hand and grabbed for the hem of her shirt. "Last one in—"

Nick grabbed her hands, halting their upward progress. "What are you doing?"

"It's okay, he's out of town for the week." She pushed his hands away and ripped her tank top over her head, tossing it onto one of the lounge chairs. "Are you coming in, or not?"

"Not."

She shrugged, her breasts bobbing up and down. "Suit yourself." Then she toed off her boots and shimmied out of her cut-offs. Once she was naked, she stood in front of him. "Don't you wanna?" Lacey grabbed his hand and pressed it to one of her breasts. "See? I'm hot. You're hot. This will cool us down."

"It's not our pool. It belongs to the judge."

"He'll never know." She trailed his hand down her torso to the triangle of curls at the juncture of her thighs. "I promise not to scream."

When he didn't move, she dropped his hand and turned her back on him. "Skinny-dippin' is more fun with two."

NICK'S BREATH caught and held as Lacey entered the water, one step at a time. Moonlight glinted off the rippling water and her hair, casting a pale blue glow over her skin. When she was thigh-deep, she turned and faced him.

Despite his best intentions to keep the walk platonic, Nick couldn't stop himself from ripping his shirt over his head.

He could tell when she smiled. The moonlight lit up her white teeth.

"Damn it, Lacey, I wasn't going to do anything with you tonight."

"You don't have to, just come for a swim." She stepped out farther, the water coming up to that sexy dark triangle of curls.

Nick groaned. If he got naked and in the water with Lacey, there was only one way it would go.

The boots came off next and the jeans followed.

"Now you're living." Lacey pushed off from the bottom and swam to the end of the pool.

Nick stepped into the water, his dick as hard as concrete, his body on fire. The cool water did nothing to temper the molten blood flowing through his veins, but it felt good.

"Ever been skinny-dipping?" Lacey floated on her back, moonbeams kissing her face and breasts.

"When I was a kid."

"Never as an adult?" She clucked her tongue. "Although I have to admit, it's been a long time since I have."

"Did you ever skinny-dip with your ex?"

She laughed. "Are you kidding? He would have been appalled at the thought, much less the act." Lacey moved her arms, sending her body in a straight line toward him. "I like swimming naked. There's something to be said for being naughty. It turns me on."

Nick's hands scooped beneath her bottom so that she stayed floating on top of the water. "*You* turn me on."

Her brows rose. "Do I?" She reached below the surface, her hand coming in contact with his engorged member. "I do, don't I?" A smile lit her face, her teeth shining in the night. "So what are you going to do about it?" Her fingers closed around him. "And don't say nothing, because you know you want to."

"Is everything about sex with you?"

"No, sometimes it's about taking walks with handsome cowboy-mechanics." She arched her back, her breasts rising up from the water, tempting him.

Past the ability to resist her, Nick bent to take one luscious, wet nipple between his lips. With one of his hands firmly attached to her bottom, keeping her afloat, Nick raised his other hand to skim across her flat belly.

"Hmm. I like this." Lacey let her legs float apart, her free hand rising to guide his hand lower.

Nick threaded his fingers through the tuft of curls, parting her folds. He tapped the little nubbin, flicking it softly.

"That's it. There." She let go of him and swept her hand to the side, positioning herself with her back to the side of the pool. She grasped the edge and held on.

Nick moved between her legs, ducking low in the water until he draped her thighs over his shoulders.

"Isn't this much better than lying in a hot bed, sweltering in the heat?" she whispered.

"Much." He tongued her pussy, swirling around the opening then moving up to her clit, flicking it again and again until she moaned softly.

"That feels soooo good." She writhed in the water, her legs alternately clenching around his ears and falling open, her heels digging into his back.

Her body grew more tense, her muscles tightening and her movements coming in short jerks. "Oh sweet Jesus, you know what it takes." Her words were strained. She let go of the edge of the pool with one hand and gripped a handful of his hair, holding him steady, urging him to take more, move faster.

He obliged.

When she stopped moving, her breath caught and held, her fingers pulling tight enough his scalp ached, he knew he had her where he wanted her.

"Now. I want you inside me now."

"I don't have protection."

"I'm on the damned pill." She slid her legs off his shoulders and touched bottom, then grabbed his hand and led him toward the steps. "I need that big dick. Now."

He chuckled, the sound more like a cough in his tight chest. He wanted to fuck her hard and fast. Julia had never been into manic sex, the kind that left you breathing hard and sore from pounding. She'd been too worried about messing up the sheets. And she hadn't liked how big his cock was, complaining that he'd hurt her if he went faster or harder.

When Lacey reached the steps, she bent over, raising her ass in the water to the level he could manage. She had no qualms about hot jackhammer sex.

Nick grabbed her hips and rammed his cock deep inside her.

"Yesss." Lacey moaned and leaned into him, taking him deeper. "Fuck me, grease monkey. Ride me like a Harley. Give me some great monkey sex."

Nick laughed out loud, then clamped a hand over his mouth, remembering too late that he was trespassing in the district court judge's pool. "We're going to jail."

"Well then fuck me like it's your last time before they mark you as a pretty boy and make you do it with all the hard-case criminals behind bars."

He slapped her ass. "That's not doing it for me. Come up with something sexier."

Her back arched. "Your cock is so big, it fills me so tight, I could die like this."

"Don't. I'd have a tough time explaining why I'm doing a dead woman in the judge's pool." He grabbed her hair and tugged on it, pulling her back. "Do you like that?"

"Oh, yes. A little pain makes it all the more exciting." She raised and lowered herself on him. "Pound me, grease monkey. Make me squeal."

"Hey, you promised not to scream."

"I lied."

"Yup, I'm going to jail." He pulled free and stood her on her feet in front of him. "If I'm going to jail, at least give me the satisfaction of seeing your face as you lose it."

Lacey smiled and pressed a kiss to his lips, deepening it as she wrapped her legs around him.

Nick gripped her hips and slammed her down over him.

Lacey's head dropped back and she let out a soft squeal. "Oh, dear God, yes!"

The way she scrunched her eyes closed and the caress of her hands sliding across his back as she rode him, added to the exquisite feeling of being inside her tight channel, his cock throbbing against the slick walls of her pussy.

Nick pitched over the edge, his body growing rigid, his seed shooting inside her.

For a long moment he held her, half in and half out

of the water. He'd never made love to a woman quite like that and it felt so good, he wanted to shout.

When his muscles finally began to relax, he leaned away from her. "Are you all right?"

She sighed, her eyes drooping. "Better than all right. Want me to get down?" Her ankles remained locked behind him.

His cock waned inside her. "Not unless you want to."

She stiffened. "We might consider running about now."

Nick stared down at her. Was this another one of her naughty tricks? "What do you mean?"

"I see a beam of light shining through the hedges, and if I'm not mistaken, there are blue lights flashing on the other side of the judge's house."

"Holy shit!" Nick shoved Lacey out of the water onto the deck surrounding the pool and climbed out beside her. In a flurry of movement, he gathered her clothing and his and made a dash for the hedges on the other side of the house, away from the flashlight now shining on the pool.

"Halt! Police!"

Unwilling to face the music naked, Nick shoved through the bushes, dragging a giggling Lacey behind him.

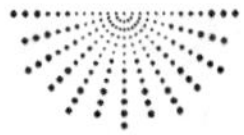

CHAPTER EIGHT

"Sounds to me like you're falling hard for Nick," Kendall teased Lacey the next day at work.

"I'm not falling in love with anyone." Lacey set a twelve-pack of long-neck beer on the floor beside Kendall.

"What's it going to take for you to get over your ex and move on?" Kendall stood with one hand on her hip. "I keep telling you, not all men are assholes."

"It'll take a knight on a white horse charging in to sweep me off my feet in the middle of one of the Temptation Garden Club meetings." Lacey pointed at the twelve-pack. "That's not getting into the cooler by itself."

"Is that all? A knight on a white horse?" Kendall shook her head and bent to grab two bottles. "Keep dreaming, girl."

"Speaking of the Temptation Garden Club, are you going with me to the next meeting?"

"Why do you even bother?" Kendall set the bottles in the cooler behind the bar. "Those women don't give a damn about you. They're just a gossiping bunch of old biddies who don't have anything better to do."

Lacey's lips tightened. "I don't know why I still go. I guess I don't like admitting defeat to anyone, especially them."

"Defeat?" Kendall stepped back, a frown creasing her brow. "That bastard cheated on you. How is that defeat?"

"I didn't hold my marriage together. He wasn't getting what he wanted from our relationship."

"Because he was a class-A dick." Kendall rolled her eyes and reached for more bottles. "Not because you were at fault."

"Still, if I quit going, it'll look like I'm slinking away with my tail between my legs."

"I'll be there." Kendall slammed the cooler shut. "When is it?"

"Saturday."

"Saturday?" Kendall's face fell. "Damn it."

Lacey's chest tightened. "You have other plans?" It had been two months since she'd been to the last meeting by herself and she didn't look forward to going into the lions' den without a little moral support from a friend.

"I told Ed I'd go to Dallas with him. He's looking at a stallion that day." She wiped her hands on a bar towel. "I'll tell him I can't go with him."

"No. You need to go with Ed. He's your number-one priority now." Lacey forced a smile she didn't feel. She couldn't drag Kendall into her life when she had one of her own to lead with Ed.

"I wouldn't dream of letting you go back to that horde of back-stabbing bitches without me to watch your back."

"I can manage just fine." Maybe she'd skip after all. The thought of going alone held no appeal, even if it was to save face.

"No way." Kendall hugged Lacey. "I'll talk with Ed."

Lacey grabbed Kendall's arms and gave her a stern look. "Don't you dare. I assure you I'll be fine."

Kendall's eyes narrowed. "Are you sure? Or are you blowing smoke up my shorts just to make me feel better?"

"I'm sure." Lacey patted Kendall's shoulders and spun her away. "Now, go get those other twelve-packs of beer. The doors open in fifteen."

The night passed without incident. In Lacey's books, anyway. Neither Cory nor Nick showed up. Only one barroom fight, with minimal damage to the premises, and one call to the police. No guys came into the Ugly Stick who interested Lacey enough to flirt with.

She watched the door the entire evening all the way to closing time.

Audrey slipped an arm around Lacey's shoulders as she placed the last clean beer mug on the shelf. "Go home, girl. It's been a long night."

"You're telling me." Lacey sighed. The thought of going back to her apartment and lying down on her bed alone held absolutely no appeal. Maybe she'd stop by Judge Stephens's place and take a dip in his pool. "See ya tomorrow. Remember I'll be in late on Saturday."

"That's right. You have that garden thing to go to." Audrey shook her head. "I can't see you rubbing elbows with the matrons of Temptation in a stuffy garden party." She shrugged. "But whatever blows your skirts up is fine with me. Night."

Lacey grabbed her purse and keys from under the counter and slipped into her car. By the time she got to the apartment, not a single light shone in the windows of the lower apartment.

The old house appeared closed and uninviting for the first time since she'd moved in. She trudged up the stairs, her ears perked for a voice, a sign that someone wasn't as asleep as they appeared, but not a sound came from the apartment below.

The air in her apartment was stale, stuffy and smelled of old building. Lacey crossed to the window and slid it open enough to allow the night breeze to enter and refresh the room. She stood looking out across the street at the sleeping houses of the neighborhood as she stripped out of her clothes. For a moment, she stood naked in front of her window, daring someone to wake up and stare back or even yell for her to put some clothes on.

No one did.

After a minute or two, she ducked into a lukewarm shower, toweled off and lay down on her bed, the cool sheets caressing her bare skin. She was tired to the bone. Too tired to even switch on her vibrator.

She laid her arm over her eyes to block out the moon shining through her open curtains. For a long moment, she remained still, waiting…for what?

When she finally gave up on sleep, she reached into her nightstand, yanked out her vibrator and tipped the on switch, setting it into motion. If she couldn't have sex with a real man, the silver, bullet-shaped little gadget would have to do.

Lying back on the bed, she slipped the cool metal cylinder down the column of her throat, over her collarbone and lower to the tip of one of her breasts. The nipple peaked and knotted into a tight little bead.

Good. But not as good as being with *him.*

She refused to name the *him* in her mind, but images of Nick in his coveralls, Nick in a towel and Nick naked couldn't be erased as easily. As she eased the vibrator downward, over her belly to the thatch of curls over her pussy, she moaned, splaying her knees to the side.

If *he* was there, he'd go down on her, draping her thighs over his shoulders, spreading her open and licking her clit in long, luscious strokes.

Lacey parted her folds with her fingertips and touched the throbbing machine to that special bundle of excitable nerves.

At a single touch, she arched her back off the mattress and dug her heels into the mattress, a louder moan rising from her throat. She closed her eyes and allowed herself to sink deeper into the fantasy of being taken by the cowboy. "Yes, there."

He'd be wearing his overalls and cowboy boots and nothing else. That way when she slipped the zipper down, she could run her hand across his chest and down to capture his…

She rammed the vibrator into her entrance, the hum of the motor and the sensations it inspired spreading little electrical shocks along all of her nerve endings. Tingling began in her toes and fingers, racing along her system to pool at her core.

Lusty juices oozed from her entrance as she dipped the device in and out of her then up to slide across her clit. "Yes!" she said out loud. "More, please."

Her imaginary mechanic pumped in and out of her, his dick hard and smooth like metal, only too thin to be real and too cold to make her crazy. After several hard thrusts, Lacey shoved the vibrator to the side, a sob rising in her throat.

Being single and free had its advantages, but lying in a cold bed by herself wasn't one of them. She longed for strong arms to circle her, a warm body spooning her and a big, hard dick driving in and out until she couldn't stand it anymore. And not just anybody. She wanted Nick, and no vibrator would take his place.

For a long time she lay in her bed, staring up at the ceiling, sleep a long way from coming.

She'd done it. Lacey Lambert had fallen for a cowboy whose own hang-ups equaled if not exceeded her own. "Hell."

NICK KNEW EXACTLY when Lacey made it back to the apartment. He'd been pacing the apartment from the time he got home from the shop to the time Lacey drove up in the driveway. When Lacey didn't stop at his door, Nick stripped out of his clothes, took an icy-cold shower and walked naked into his bedroom, where he lay across the sheets, praying his cock would ease up.

It stood for over an hour at attention, eager to find Lacey and thrust deep inside her.

So why was Nick holding back? He liked her. Hell, he found her exciting and uninhibited and everything his ex hadn't been…with him.

Perhaps Cory was right. Not all women were the same and not all relationships ended the same. Yet the residual anger of his divorce left him clenching the bedsheets instead of following the woman up the stairs and burying himself deep inside her. Well past two, he lay awake, but he must have fallen asleep because when he opened his eyes again, sun poured through his window.

He stretched, his naked skin skimming across twisted sheets, his normal boner as hard as it had been last night when he'd wished he'd gone up to the neighbor's apartment.

A glance at the clock reminded him of his responsibilities. He was already an hour late to open the shop. Nick got up and slipped into a set of coveralls and zipped them up to his waist, leaving the top hanging around his hips. His dick made a tent of the fabric and he thanked the uniform company for recommending he buy the coveralls a size larger.

Barefoot, he walked across the apartment to the kitchen. The place was dead quiet. A note on the counter indicated Cory had left an hour ago for a term exam and wouldn't be back until that afternoon.

Footsteps above made Nick glance at the ceiling, his hand rising to cup his throbbing dick.

By the sounds of it, Lacey was awake and moving around up there. Lust spiked and his cock hardened even more. Would she be in the mood for a little morning fuck?

Nick shook his head. Only a jerk would rush up the stairs and ask that. He stared at the kitchen, his mind on the apartment above.

What about breakfast? He could ask if she'd like breakfast. That was a neutral request, no strings, just food.

He spun on his heel and marched across the floor to the door, reaching out for the handle.

Before he could twist it, a soft knock sounded.

A grin spread across Nick's face. It had to be Lacey.

He whipped the door open, his smile sliding downward.

"Julia. What are you doing here?" He glanced over her shoulder to the staircase.

Her brows rose and she slipped past him into his apartment before she turned to face him again. "Expecting someone else?"

Nick glanced at the steps again then faced his ex-wife. "What do you want, Julia? You already have half of everything I ever earned."

"I don't want anything, Nicky baby." She stepped up to him and ran her finger along his jawline. "I missed you. Is that a crime?"

He captured her wrist in his hand and held it away from him. "Julia, you're a fuckin' moving violation. Leave."

"I just got here, sweetheart." She pulled her hand free and backed deeper into the apartment, finally settling on the couch. "Come." Julia patted the cushion beside her. "Sit and talk to me for old times' sake."

"We have absolutely nothing to talk about." Nick remained at the door, his eyes narrowed, wondering what he'd ever seen in Julia.

Sure, she was beautiful with her long honey-blond hair lying in smooth waves around her shoulders. She kept her figure trim with a personal trainer and every kind of diet ever imagined. But her blue eyes were cold, lacking the warmth and twinkle he'd come to admire in…

"Did your gardener leave you?"

"Tim?" She waved a hand as if dismissing the younger man she'd had an affair with. "We were never a big thing."

"Fucking him in my bed was a big thing to me."

"Oh, Nicky, darling, you're not still mad about that, are you?" Julia rose and crossed to where Nick still stood and rested her hand on his bare chest.

"Julia, we're divorced. You shouldn't be here. You should be with Tom, or Bob or whatever his name is."

"Tim isn't a part of my life. He was never as good in bed as you were."

"So sorry to hear you traded down in the dick department." The tiny pout on her lips that used to make him do anything for her now only made him mad.

Nick recognized it as the pout of a child who was used to getting her own way. He liked a woman who earned her way in the world. One who didn't take advantage of a man's good intentions. Nick stepped back and jabbed a thumb toward the door. "Get out."

"Oh, Nicky baby, you don't mean that?" She stepped up to him again, walking her fingers up his chest to tap one against his lips. "Don't you miss me? Even a little bitty bit?" Julia leaned up on her toes and puckered her lips to kiss him.

"Nick have you seen my crystal-studded purple panties?" Lacey sailed through his open apartment door completely naked, her long dark hair bouncing around her shoulders, a twinkle in her deep brown eyes. She stopped at the couch and bent to lift a cushion, her beautiful full ass shining in Julia's face. "I swear I was wearing them last night before you, me and Cory had sex here on the couch." Lacey shoved the cushions back in place and straightened. "Or was it while we were doing it in the kitchen?" Her search moved to the kitchen.

Laughter threatened to bubble up in Nick's chest.

"You had sex with Nick...*and* Cory?" Julia's eyes rounded, her mouth falling open in a very unattractive gape. Her gaze moved from Nick to Lacey and back. "I don't understand."

"She's not too bright, is she?" Lacey faced Julia, giving the other woman a full-on view of her beautiful curves. "Nick, Cory and I have been having wall-banging sex since they moved in." Lacey's gaze traveled Julia's length. "I take it you're Nick's ex?"

Julia nodded, wordlessly.

Lacey's brows rose. "And you never had sex with both of them?" She clucked her tongue. "Missed an opportunity there. They're pretty good." Lacey grabbed for something on the counter. "There they are." She held out her hand, a bright pair of purple panties hanging from her finger. "Spent all my stripper tips on that pair. Would hate to lose them." She sauntered back across the room and paused in front of Nick. "See you at lunch? I've always wanted to do it in a mechanic's shop." Without missing a beat, she rubbed the panties along Nick's jaw. "What's it like, Jane?"

"Julia…my n-name is Julia," Nick's ex stuttered. "And I wouldn't know."

With her arm around Nick's neck, her breasts pressed against his chest and her crotch straddling one of his thighs, Lacey looked over her shoulder. "You never did it in his shop?"

"Of course not." Julia pushed back her shoulders. "It's so dirty."

"Haven't you ever had dirty sex?" Lacey slipped her hand into the front of Nick's coveralls and gripped his engorged cock. "Stick around. I'll show you how it's done."

Her face flaming bright red, Julia backed toward the door. "I never—"

Nick would have laughed out loud, but Lacey had hold of his dick and he couldn't think past how good it felt.

"Maybe you should have." Lacey clasped Nick's

zipper with her free hand and pulled it down with slow deliberation.

Julia squealed and darted out the door, slamming it behind her.

Nick forced a grin and kissed Lacey's nose. "Thanks."

"For what?" She pushed the coveralls down over his hips.

"For getting rid of my ex."

"Oh, her?" She marched her finger up his chest, much like Julia had, and touched his lip. "She didn't bother me a bit."

"Well, she was bothering me." He caught her finger and held it close, pressing a kiss to the tip. "You don't have to pretend anymore."

"Who said I was pretending?" Her gaze captured his. "I didn't sleep at all last night."

Nick's pulse raced, his groin tightening. "Funny. Neither did I." He slipped an arm around her waist and crushed her to his chest. "Wanna know why?"

"I can guess." Her hand tightened around his cock, easing it from the confines of his coveralls.

"You're making me insane." Nick grabbed her thighs and hiked her up, wrapping her legs around him.

"Ditto." Lacey lowered herself over his cock, taking him in, her eyes fluttering closed. "My vibrator just isn't cutting it."

"Was that the humming sound I heard on the ceiling?"

"Yeah, it fell on the floor." Lacey kissed his temple.

Nick liked it when she did that. Her lips were soft, yet firm, pliable but strong when wrapped around his…

"Wouldn't we be more comfortable on the couch?" she suggested.

"Or in my bed?"

"Now you're talking."

"Ah, hell, I can't wait another second." He didn't take a step toward the bedroom. Instead, he leaned Lacey's back into the wall and held onto her thighs as he thrust in and out of her.

She wrapped her hands around his neck and rode him, her head thrown back, her breasts bobbing in his face. "Much…better…than…vibrator." Her words ended on a scream, her fingernails digging into his shoulders.

When he shot to the edge and over, Nick thrust once more, his cock sinking deep inside her hot, slick channel. He squeezed his eyes shut, the excruciating beauty of their connection robbing him of breath. His dick throbbed inside her. As he returned to his apartment living room, he reached out and nipped one of her nipples.

Lacey batted at him. "Hey, what was that for?"

"Making me lose it before I can make you happy."

"Oh, honey, I'm happy all right." She locked her ankles behind his back.

"But it can and will be better." He clamped his arms around her waist and carried her into his bedroom, laying her across the mattress.

"Don't you have some cars to tinker with?" she asked, her knees dropping over the edge of the mattress.

"I'm my own boss. I can set my own hours. And I have some work to do here."

"Oh, so I'm work, am I?" She pushed up on her elbows.

"The best kind of work there is." Nick leaned over her, his cock skimming across her belly as he pressed her shoulders to the mattress and a kiss to her lips. "Trust me."

"Show me that I can," she whispered, her brown-eyed gaze staring up into his.

The way she said the words struck home to him. She was a woman who played hard and fast. Why? Because she'd been hurt before and maybe her need to hit and run came from fear.

"I'll prove it to you." He kissed a path down the long line of her neck, capturing a peaked nipple between his teeth. "Trust me yet?"

"Hardly." Her fingers laced in his hair, guiding him lower. "Show me more."

"As you wish." Nick slipped his lips along her rib cage, nipping the skin and tasting his way across her contours, leading to the triangle of curls hiding her mons. "Here's where I seal the deal."

"Yeah, yeah," she said, her voice strained. "All talk, no act—"

He tongued her clit with the slightest of taps.

Lacey's back arched off the bed, her heels pressing into the mattress, her hips rising to his mouth. "Oh, sweet Jesus!"

"Trust me now?"

"I trust that you can make me squeal." She gripped his hair and shoved him close. "Don't stop now."

He flicked the tender nubbin of nerves again.

Lacey cried out. "I'm going to come!" Her muscles tightened, her breath caught in her lungs and she pulled so hard on Nick's hair he feared it might come out. "Stop. No don't."

He continued his attack on her sweet spot, sending her flying over the edge, a thin sheen of perspiration coating her body, her eyes closed tightly, her lips pinched together.

Finally, she settled back against the comforter, her fingers loosening in his hair, smoothing down over his shoulders.

Nick climbed up on the bed beside her and spooned her back against his front, his dick, losing its hardness, pressed to her back.

Lacey reached behind her, cupping his ass. "Mind-blowing."

"The sex?" Nick chuckled. "You deserved it."

She stilled, her fingernails digging into his buttocks. "That wasn't thank-you sex, was it?"

He pushed the hair away from her neck and kissed her. "Not at all." Nick chuckled. "Though the look on Julia's face when you walked in here naked was priceless."

"You wouldn't lie to me, would you?" Lacey waited for his answer.

"I would never lie to you, Lacey." He tightened his arms around her middle and fit her snuggly against his body. "You're an amazing woman and your ex didn't deserve you."

"Right answer." She relaxed in his arms, her breathing returning to normal. "What am I going to do with you?"

His cock twitched between her butt cheeks. "More of what we just did?" he suggested.

"You mean you have something left in you?" She turned in his embrace. "Hmmm, you do." She draped a leg over his hip, rubbing her damp pussy against his thigh. "I think I can muster up some energy."

She touched his cock and it sprang back to life.

As Nick embarked on another earth-shattering orgasm, he wondered what was next in his relationship with Lacey. He was certain that letting her walk out of his life at this point was not an option.

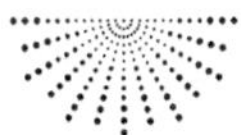

CHAPTER NINE

*L*acey left Nick and Cory's apartment an hour later, walking up the steps a little stiffly, her legs strained from riding her cowboy for the second time that day. When she pushed through her door, she gasped.

"Took you long enough." Kendall leaned against the back of the couch, her cowboy boot tapping against the wooden floor. "From all the noise you two were making down there, you'd have thought it was an orgy. How many of the McBrides were you onto?"

"Just one." Lacey passed by Kendall on her way to her bedroom, a smile tilting her lips. "Not that it's any of your business."

Kendall followed. "Which one?"

"Like I said, it's not—"

"Bullshit." Kendall grabbed Lacey's shoulders. "If it's Cory, be careful. He's young and impressionable."

"Relax. Cory is safely away from this cougar and working hard at his studies in college."

Kendall's grip relaxed and she pulled Lacey into a hug. "Thank God."

A nudge of anger spiked in Lacey and she struggled out of Kendall's embrace. "You'd think you were the boy's mother."

"I wasn't thanking God about Cory. I was thanking Him for giving you another chance to find love."

A hammer slammed into her chest. Kendall's straightforward statement hit her hard and almost brought her to her knees.

"Don't know what you're talking about." She ducked into the bedroom, refusing to meet Kendall's gaze. In love with Nick? That would be the height of stupidity. She'd been naive enough to fall for Randy and all his lies. She couldn't put herself through that again. "No," she whispered, reaching out to the wall to steady herself when her knees threatened to buckle.

"I know what you're thinking." Kendall leaned against the doorframe.

"So now you're a mind-reader?" Lacey straightened her shoulders, grabbed fresh panties and a bra and entered the bathroom, hoping to shake the other woman off and avoid any pointed questions she couldn't answer. Not now. Not after having the best sex of her life. Even more the walk they'd taken in the moonlight, without sex...well until they'd taken a devious dip in the judge's pool. A warm flush washed over her. And then there was this morning...

Lacey flipped the handle for the shower, sending a cool, steady stream into the tub. Cool showers were becoming a habit when she thought about Nick.

"Doesn't take much to read your mind."

"Really?" Lacey stepped into the tub and closed the shower curtain, glad for a shield between her and Kendall. Her friend read far too much into her facial expressions.

"Yeah. You're in love with Nick."

Lacey's gut clenched, her eyes stinging with unshed tears. She pounded her fist against the cool tile wall. "I can't be in love."

"What did you say?"

Lacey leaned into the spray, the water doing little to cool the heat radiating from her entire body. "I've only really known him a couple days. It doesn't make sense to think I could fall in love that quickly."

"My parents knew each other less than a week before they decided to get married. Love has a way of finding you, especially when you're not looking for it."

Lacey forced a chuckle when a sob was what wanted to come out. "Oh wise one, tell me what I'm supposed to do with this newfound knowledge." What the hell was she supposed to do? If Kendall was right—and if the way her heart beat whenever she saw Nick across a room was any indication—and she was in love with Nick—holy hell!

Kendall ripped the curtain aside, one corner of her mouth quirked upward. "Go with it, Lacey. Give him a chance. Hell, give yourself a chance."

As she stared across at her friend, tears slipping from the corners of her eyes, Lacey shook her head. "I can't."

"Why not?" Kendall smiled. "He's a good guy."

"I told him I didn't want strings. And I didn't." Lacey stared down at her hands.

"Then tell him you were wrong."

How in hell had she gotten so close to Nick? "He's not interested."

"Oh yeah? He's been into the bar the past few nights. He never came to the Ugly Stick before he met you."

"He's divorced. He's probably lonely and looking for a little companionship."

"He came in looking for you, dufus." Kendall laughed. "And you were looking for him." She held up her hand. "And don't tell me you weren't. You dropped bottles, spilled drinks and nearly tripped over every pair of cowboy boots in the place watching the door for him to walk in." Kendall patted her chest. "I saw it. Audrey sees it. Hell, anyone with eyes at the Ugly Stick could see it."

Lacey pressed her palms to her face. "Everybody?" Her cheeks burned. "Was it that obvious?"

"Yes, chica. But don't get your back up. We love you and want you to be happy." Kendall turned off the water and handed her a towel. "So, if the man makes a move toward a permanent relationship, don't push him away."

"I won't have to. He won't." Lacey patted her body with the towel and swiped at the tears that continued to fall, despite her resolve to never cry over a man. "We made an agreement up front. No strings."

Kendall took the towel, turned Lacey away from her and squeezed the water out of Lacey's long hair. "Then rewrite the agreement."

Lacey spun to face Kendall. "I've been burned by a man before. It really hurts."

"Don't judge all men by Randy's standards." Kendall brushed the towel over Lacey's breast. "Nick's a good guy." She shoved the towel into Lacey's arms. "Now finish drying and dressing before I call Ed in for another nooner. Damn, woman, you make me hot." Kendall left the bathroom, closing the door behind her.

Lacey smiled, her tears drying, her thoughts on Nick in the apartment below.

Could she really walk in there and ask him to change the rules this late in the game?

Was this warm, sometimes-painful yearning really love or just a brief infatuation?

She raked a brush through her hair, slipped into her panties and bra and flung open the door. "I'll do it."

Kendall sat on the edge of her bed, her slim, shapely legs crossed. "Of course you will. You're the one who taught me to take chances for the one I loved and look where it got me." She grinned. "I now have the sexiest cowboy in the tri-county area."

"Do you think Nick will run the other way?"

"You won't know until you try." Kendall jerked her head toward the door. "Go on, get down there and see where you stand with the man."

Lacey hurried toward the door, forcing reason to the back of her mind, running on nothing but hope.

"Wait." Kendall's voice called her back.

"What?"

"Put some clothes on. You want him to love you for you, not for a quick fuck." Kendall tossed her a tank top and cutoff jeans. "Not that these are any less revealing than what you have on. But you don't want to appear *too* eager to take things to the next level."

Lacey jammed her feet into the shorts and slipped the tank over her head. "When did you get to be so smart?"

"I had a good teacher's assistant in my sex education lessons, sweetie." Kendall gave her a gentle shove toward the door. "Go get 'em, tiger."

Lacey raced down to the bottom of the stairs and paused with her knuckles hovering over the wood-paneled door. What was she thinking?

"Do it," Kendall urged from the landing above.

Closing her eyes, Lacey knocked. Her breath caught in her throat and she willed the door to open. *Please, please, please.* Before she lost her nerve.

Footsteps echoed across the wood floor on the other side.

Her heart pumping hard in her chest, Lacey waited to open her eyes until she heard the squeak of the hinges.

Her eyes opened at the same time as the door.

"Lacey. What are you doing here?"

Her heart fell lower than her belly and she gulped back the knot forming in her throat. "Oh, hi, Cory. Is Nick here?"

"As a matter of fact he isn't. He got word just a

moment ago that his house is finished. He'll be moving in this afternoon." Cory grinned. "Perhaps I can help you." He held the door wide. "Come in."

Lacey raised a hand to her throat, air refusing to move in and out of her lungs. "Moving? He didn't tell me he was moving." A sinking feeling hit the pit of her stomach. Perhaps he hadn't mentioned the move because he didn't want to see her again.

"Yeah, this arrangement—him living with me—was only temporary until the contractors finished his house on the ranch he bought." Cory's eyes narrowed. "Are you okay?"

"No." She backed away. "I mean yes."

"Want to leave a message? He'll be back later to pack up."

She shook her head, willing the tears not to fall. "No. It wasn't important."

"Are you working the Ugly Stick tonight?" Cory asked.

Lacey's head moved up and down automatically.

"Good. I could use all the moral support from my friends since it's Ladies' Night." Cory's brows dipped. "Are you sure you don't want to leave a message for my big brother?"

"No. I have to go." Lacey turned and raced up the stairs and into her apartment before the dam burst and she lost it. So much for running on a hunch.

"What happened?" Kendall closed the door behind her. "What did he say?" She bunched her fists. "Did that bastard make you cry?"

Lacey stood in the middle of the room, staring around at what had once been her haven and now looked more like an empty shell of a room. "He wasn't there."

"Then you can tell him tonight after you get off work."

"He won't be there."

"What do you mean?"

"He's moving out."

"Well, that only makes it a bit more of a challenge." Kendall pulled her into her arms. "You're tough. You can handle it."

"I don't know. Maybe it wasn't meant to be."

"Don't go all Debbie-downer on me. Give the guy a chance."

"Shouldn't he be coming to me?"

"Did I wait for Ed to come chasing after me?" Kendall poked a finger at Lacey's chest. "On advice of a really good friend, I went after him. And I got him."

Lacey sucked in a deep breath and let it out on a sigh. "Not every fairytale has a happy ending."

NICK SPENT a couple hours at the shop, interviewing mechanics and making the repairs he'd promised. Before long, he'd be working the ranch and he'd only drop into the shop every so often as the owner, not the chief mechanic. The work had given him the outlet he'd needed to burn off his anger and rebuild his confidence. But now that his house was finished, he could spend his days working with horses he hoped to buy soon and cattle he planned to fill the pastures with. He'd finally have what he'd always dreamed of…a ranch and a place to call home.

It had only taken one load to empty his belongings out of Cory's apartment. The rest of his stuff had been consigned to a storage shed and Cory helped him move the items using a U-Haul and Nick's pickup truck.

Nick stood in the spacious living room with the cathedral ceilings and huge windows overlooking the pastures to the south. The folding chairs did nothing for the ambiance, but as soon as he could, he'd shop for furniture to fill his home.

Cory stood beside him. "Wow, this place is big compared to my little apartment."

"You're welcome to stay here with me."

"I might take you up on that on the weekends and summer break. But for now, the apartment in town is more convenient to my college."

"Thanks for helping me."

"Yeah, anytime. Now I have to get going. It's Ladies' Night at the Ugly Stick and I need to wax my chest."

Nick snorted. "Like you have any chest hair."

Cory's lips twisted. "I have a few." His gaze spanned the living room. "You sure you're not going to get lonely out here?"

"I'll be fine." Damn Cory for nailing the exact thought Nick had been avoiding. "Before long, I'll be too busy to be lonely."

"You should bring Lacey out here to see this. I bet she'd love it."

Nick shrugged. "I'd think it would be too homey for her. She might think I wanted her to stay." *Forever.*

Cory nodded. "She did say she wasn't into commitment."

"She did." Nick shoved his hands into his pockets.

"I wonder if she really meant it."

Nick had wondered that himself. He'd told her in no uncertain terms that he wasn't in the market for a permanent relationship, but lately, he found his resolve slipping. "Why wouldn't she mean it?"

"Just saying…" Cory nodded toward the bedrooms. "What are you going to do for a bed to sleep on?"

"Jackson and Audrey got a new one last week and offered to sell me their old one. I expect them to be here any minute."

"I'll stay to help unload, then I really have to go get ready."

Nick's lips twitched. "I wouldn't dream of standing in the way of a man and his wax job."

"Hey, don't knock it." Cory ran his hands across his chest and down his belly. "These abs are paying my way through school."

"I told you I'd foot the bill for your tuition."

"Yeah, but I'm glad I can do it myself. Makes me appreciate it more and actually study."

"Good point. Let me know if you need anything. I'm doing pretty good with my investment portfolio."

"Remind me to get with you when I've saved enough tips to start my own investments."

"You got it."

"Hello?" Audrey's voice echoed through the hallway.

She appeared around the corner carrying a potted plant. "There you are. Jackson's untying the load on his truck."

"I'll help." Cory left the room.

When Nick started to follow, Audrey laid a hand on his arm, balancing the plant in the other. "Wait. I have something I want to say."

Nick smiled down at her. "Shoot."

"First, this is a house-warming gift." She set the plant on the floor. "Remember to water it at least once a week."

"Thanks." Nick stared at the plant, waiting for Audrey to get to the real point.

And she did. "I'm worried about Lacey."

His heart flipped over and thumped hard against his ribs. "What's wrong with Lacey?"

"She's not been herself lately and it's not like her."

Nick frowned. "What do you want me to do about it? I'm not her keeper."

"I know that." Audrey laughed. "No one is Lacey's keeper. She's a force unto herself. Still I can't help but think you two are perfect for each other."

Nick backed away. "We're just friends." *With benefits.*

Audrey's brows rose. "I've seen the way you look at her. It's not a friendly look. It's one suited more to a man in love."

What was with everyone talking about love? "I'm not in love with Lacey."

"Tell yourself whatever you want, I can see it in your eyes." She shook her head. "I'm just afraid you two are going to miss out on a happily ever after if you don't pull your heads out of your…well, you get the picture." She crossed her arms.

"I should help the guys unload the truck." Nick edged away from her.

"Let me tell you one more thing. It'll take a lot of convincing to get Lacey to believe in love again. She was hurt pretty badly when her husband cheated on her. She had a lot of dreams about love and marriage that went up in smoke the day the Temptation Garden Club ladies felt it was their duty to burst her bubble in front of everyone."

"I'm sorry she was hurt." And he really was. Lacey deserved a lot better than what those snooty bitches gave her. He'd even heard through his clients about the incident, not knowing Lacey at the time. They'd been ruthless, mean-spirited and ugly to her. No one should be subjected to that kind of public flogging. "But I don't understand what this has to do with me."

"As I was saying, it would take a knight on a white horse swooping in to rescue her to make her believe in love again. Just saying." She propped her hands on her hips and glanced around the room for the first time. "This is a really nice place you have here. It needs a woman and a half-dozen children running around to make it a home."

Nick chuckled. "Anyone ever tell you you're pushy?"

She gave him a wink over her shoulder. "Too many times to count. But I get what I want."

"I'll bet you do."

"Oh, and by the way, the Temptation Garden Club is sponsoring an open house at the Double Diamond

Ranch gardens tomorrow afternoon. Jackson and I will be there, and I understand Lacey will be there as well." She turned toward the exit. "That's all I had to say. Let's get you moved in." The owner of the Ugly Stick Saloon walked out of his house, leaving Nick feeling as if he'd been hit by an F-5 tornado.

"She doesn't want commitment," he called out after Audrey.

"Lacey doesn't know what she wants anymore." Audrey's disembodied voice floated to him from the front of the house. "If you were paying attention, you'd know that."

Jackson and Cory entered the living room carrying a heavy cannonball headboard.

Cory grunted under the weight. "Glad you could help."

"Had to get my marching orders from the boss first," Nick muttered.

Jackson chuckled. The Kiowa cowboy shifted the load to his other hand. "Audrey matchmaking again?" He shook his head. "Can't get that woman to quit meddling."

"Matchmaking, huh?" Cory's gaze met Nick's. "Good, someone needs to slap him upside the head so he'll pay attention."

"Nice, bro. Glad I can count on you to defend your only family," Nick groused.

"It's a king-size bed, brother." Cory moved past Nick. "Awfully big for just one person."

"Yeah." Jackson winked as he went by. "It's better

shared. We had some good times in this bed. I almost hate getting rid of it."

"Oh, quit your whining." Audrey entered the house carrying the wooden slats that would hold the mattress. "The new bed is just as big and comfortable, and prettier."

Jackson frowned. "Don't understand why we had to get rid of a perfectly good bed in the first place."

"I'm sure it will get good use in Nick's house." Audrey's gaze caught Nick's. "Won't it?"

Nick really didn't know. Would Lacey come all the way out to the ranch to visit him? Not if he didn't ask her. Did he want her in his home? He glanced at the bare wooden floors and imagined a big, soft area rug with a naked woman lying in the middle, her legs splayed wide, ready for him.

"Nick?" Cory emerged from the master bedroom. "You all right?"

Nick shook his head and adjusted his jeans. "I'm fine. Just fine."

Why was he superimposing Lacey in his new house? This house was to be his home for a very long time. If he brought a woman here, it would have to be a very special one. One he planned to have around for a long time.

"Come on, you can help me carry in the footboard." Cory draped an arm over Nick's shoulder and walked him out to Jackson's truck. "You were thinking about her, weren't you?"

"Who?" Nick played dumb. The images in his mind

refused to fade. Lacey was there, even if she wasn't physically.

"Lacey, you dumbass."

"Why is everyone trying to throw Lacey at me?" Nick pulled away from his brother. "She's not interested, I tell you."

"You won't know if you don't ask. And based on the way she looked this afternoon when she came by to see you, she's more interested than she'll admit."

"She came to see me?" Nick grabbed the front of his brother's shirt. "When? Why? What did she say?"

"Calm down." Cory pried Nick's fingers loose. "She didn't leave a message. But if it makes you feel better, she looked disappointed that I wasn't *you* when I answered the door."

"How could you tell?"

"She looked around me the entire time she stood there." Cory's eyes narrowed. "What is it with you two? You act as if you can't stand to be away from each other, but you refuse to acknowledge it. Get real and do something about it before you lose her. I kinda like the thought of having her around."

"For sex?"

"No. Not that I didn't enjoy it, but I have my eye on someone else and I'm not sure she'd like sharing. I want Lacey around to keep you from going off the deep end."

"I'm fine." Nick grabbed the end of the footboard and slid it toward him. "Just fine."

"Yeah, yeah. That's why you're about to drop that—" Cory dove for the other end of the footboard before it cleared the tailgate and crashed to the ground. "If you don't tell Lacey you're into her, I will."

"Don't you dare." Nick stared across the wooden cannonball posts. "I will when I'm ready."

"Ha!" Cory grinned. "So you admit it—you like her."

"Of course I like her." Nick walked backward toward the house, refusing to look Cory in the eye. His brother was getting too pushy. "That doesn't mean I love her."

"So what are you going to do about it?"

"Who says I have to do anything?" Nick rolled his eyes and nearly tripped over the threshold into the house.

"She needs a reminder that not all guys are jerks. Her ex played her."

"*My* ex played *me*." Nick's lips lifted on the corners. "Speaking of which, Julia came by this morning."

Cory halted, forcing Nick to stop halfway through the door. "What the hell did she want?"

"To mend fences between the two of us. She wants me back." Nick waited for his brother to explode. He wasn't disappointed.

"I hope you told the bitch to take a flying leap." Cory's eyes widened. "You aren't considering going back to her, are you? If you do, I'll disown you as a brother."

Nick's grin widened. "I didn't have to tell her where to get off. Lacey showed up."

Cory let out a long slow breath. "And?"

"Naked." Nick chuckled as he recalled the look on Julia's face when Lacey stepped through the door and bent to fish in the couch cushions for her panties that had never been there. "She was amazing."

Cory laughed out loud. "I'd have paid good money to see that. Holy hell, that woman's got balls."

Yeah, Lacey had sailed in like she owned the apartment and put Julia in her place, saving Nick from having to confront her. Hell, Lacey had saved him from Julia in more ways than one. She'd restored his faith in himself as a man and his faith in women. Some of them weren't so bad. He just had to see them through Lacey's eyes. Kendall and her willingness to share a sexual encounter with her best friend. Audrey, who would do anything for one of her girls and many of the men in her life. Not all women were lying, cheating bitches who were only looking out for themselves. "Yeah, Lacey can take care of herself and a few others along the way."

"I ask again, what are you waiting for? Tell her how you feel." Cory set the footboard on the floor of the master bedroom. "This place needs a woman. Tell her."

"Tell her what? I don't even know myself how I feel." Nick raised his hand.

"Then start there and see what happens."

Audrey poked her head in the doorway. "But be a knight on a white horse, a gentleman with enough courage to save her from herself."

"I'm beginning to feel outnumbered." Nick moaned. He knew he had to do it or kick himself from here to eternity if he didn't at least find out how she felt. "Okay. I'll talk to her."

"Don't just talk to her." Audrey lifted her arms. "Sweep her off her feet. Save her from a fate worse than death. Show her you really care." She leaned back against Jackson's big body. "You'd do that for me, wouldn't you?"

"I did when I stripped at the Ugly Stick. And I'd do it again if it meant I'd keep you forever." He wrapped his arms around her and nuzzled her neck.

Nick looked around the room, not seeing anything in it. "I need a plan."

"We can help you there," Audrey said.

CHAPTER TEN

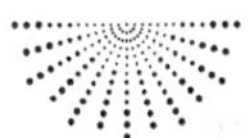

$\mathcal{L}$acey sat in her car for a long time, air conditioner cranked up to full blast, staring at the other people who were getting out of their vehicles and entering the stately double doors of the exclusive house, Double Diamond Ranch.

Every time she laid her hand on the car door handle, her breathing grew ragged and she started hyperventilating. She wished again that she'd let Kendall skip her outing with Ed in Dallas so that she would come with her to this meeting. It was at one of the Temptation Garden Club meetings that the members had informed her of her husband's infidelity and blamed her.

Lacey had come back to show them that she hadn't needed their fake pity and that she was doing great on her own. Audrey had taken her shopping, helping her pick out the perfect dress sure to raise eyebrows. In the front, the outfit was a simple, figure-hugging, tasteful design with a chaste neckline that didn't show too much cleavage. When she turned around, she expected jaws to drop and the women to gasp. The back plunged so low, if she moved just right, one could see her butt crack.

Oh, yeah, the tongues would be wagging tonight.

If she got out of the car and went inside.

She had to do this once and for all to prove to the women and to herself that she was even better off without Randy in her life and damn proud of her independence.

Then why was she wishing Nick would show up in his coveralls and offer her his arm to walk her inside?

This was ridiculous. Nick wasn't coming to her rescue. She was the only one who could rescue herself. Lacey inhaled deeply and shoved the door open, stepping out onto the lawn, her heels sinking into the earth, almost pitching her backward.

Okay, it wouldn't be good to show up in a grass-stained dress to prove a point.

She straightened and picked her way across the yard and around the side of the big house, preferring to go around to the back and enter the garden unnoticed. Recon. That's what she needed to do. See who was there and plan her next move.

Lacey stepped through a vine-covered rose arbor into the beautifully manicured garden, letting the heavenly scents of honeysuckle and roses calm her shaky nerves.

Tea tables had been set up across the smooth lawn with white umbrellas to shade the guests from the sun's dying rays. Hibiscus, mountain laurel and neatly trimmed, lush bougainvillea provided glorious bursts of color throughout the intricately designed garden. Paving stones led through a maze of bright yellow lantana, perfectly positioned limestone boulders and ruby-red crepe myrtle.

At any other time, Lacey would have enjoyed strolling through the beautiful garden. But then she spotted Randy, with an overly endowed Desiree Donnelly clinging to his arm and laughing at something Mrs. Biedel was saying.

Lacey spun on her high heels and would have left if someone hadn't hooked her arm in a firm grip.

"Lacey. You finally made it. I was looking for you." Like a steam roller, Audrey pushed her toward the crowd and the tables laden with fine finger foods. "I'm starving and I didn't want to eat alone."

"I didn't know you were a member of the Temptation Garden Club." Lacey lifted a small porcelain plate and placed a savory creampuff on it.

Her boss loaded her plate with tender chicken bites, crackers and liver pâté. "I'm not. But it's an open house, and I always wanted to get inside the Double Diamond Ranch. Haven't you?"

"Not particularly." Especially not now when her ex and his girlfriend were there. How was she supposed to look self-assured and confident when she was alone and he wasn't?

"Don't you just love the garden?"

"It's nice." Lacey laid her plate down on an empty table. "Look, Audrey, I'm not feeling very well. I think I'll go home."

Audrey's eyes widened and she glanced around the lawn as if looking for someone. "You can't. Not yet."

"Why? No one will miss me." Wasn't that the sad truth. The garden club members had never once tried to contact her to come back to a meeting. They hadn't come by with food or drinks or anything to commiserate on her husband's betrayal. As far as they were concerned she could have fallen off the face of the earth and they wouldn't have given a damn.

"I'll miss you." Audrey waved at a man coming toward them across the green grass. "And Jackson will miss you. Won't you, hon?"

"Won't I what?" He kissed Audrey and directed his attention at Lacey. "Like the dress."

"Have you seen the other side?" Audrey forced her to turn around and show off the backless side. "We figured it would make a statement."

"Uh, it has, all right. I heard a few statements from the men and their women weren't too happy about it."

Lacey pushed her shoulders back. "Good. Serves them right."

"Now you're talking like the Lacey we all know and love." Audrey patted her back. "Why don't you promenade around the garden and give the old biddies an eyeful?"

Her knees shaking, Lacey grabbed Audrey's hand. "You'll come with me?"

Jackson shook his head. "Sweetheart, you can stand on your own. You don't want to water down the effect of that dress with another person standing beside you."

He gave her nudge. "Go, strut your stuff. You've got this."

Lacey nodded. "I've got this." If she left, she'd go through life as the pathetic woman dumped by her husband and left to wallow in self-pity. She stepped out, her shoulders thrown back, her chin lifted high.

"Go, Lacey, go," Audrey called out.

She set a circuitous route around the lawn, stopping to talk with every man along the way and some of the women. As she walked on to the next group of people, she could hear the gasps and almost feel the stares of those she left gaping at her daring dress.

By the time she made it to where Randy and Desiree were talking with Mrs. Biedel, the whispers had grown louder and the entire party was talking about her dress.

Lacey pasted a huge smile on her face as she stopped beside Randy and touched his arm as if she cared. "So good to see you, Mrs. Biedel, Randy and Debbie."

"Desiree," the husband stealer said.

"Of course."

"You look like a million dollars, Lacey." Randy's gaze started at her eyes and slithered lower, lingering on her breasts and her short hemline.

"I feel like a million dollars, darling." She turned to Mrs. Biedel. "Nothing like fucking two men at once to get you in shape, right, Mrs. Biedel?"

The older woman gasped, her face turning a lovely shade of plum. "Why I wouldn't know."

"Let me be the first to apologize. I forgot to close the window the other night and I'm sure I screamed once or twice in the middle of a fabulous orgasm. I'll try to remember to close it next time."

"Please do." Mrs. Biedel fanned her face with her hand. "Is it hot out here, or is it me? I think I'll get a drink. Please excuse me."

"By all means." Lacey turned toward Randy and his date.

"Do you always go around talking about sex in such a crude manner?" Desiree asked.

Lacey smiled, feeling better than she had in months, the weight of the world slipping off her shoulders. "Do you always go around fucking other women's husbands?"

In the middle of taking a drink from a glass, Randy snorted liquid out his nose. "Lacey, have some class."

"Oh, baby, I have more class in my little finger than you have in that little bitty dick of yours. I just wanted to thank you for saving me from a fate worse than death."

"Oh really, what's that?"

"Being married to a man who doesn't know how to please a woman." She turned to Desiree, feeling sorry for the woman. "And thank you for showing me his true colors. I wish you all the best." She left the two standing with their mouths open and headed back across the yard toward Audrey and Jackson to tell them goodbye. She'd done what she'd gone there to do. Though it had given her a certain sense of satisfaction, it left her empty. She'd proven she was a strong and independent woman, but the fact was, she was going home to an empty apartment and she didn't have anyone to share a pizza with.

Before Lacey reached Audrey, Mrs. Biedel, dragging Mrs. Sandell and Mrs. Rutherford, the president and vice president of the Temptation Garden Club, stepped in front of her.

Lacey came to an abrupt halt, almost slamming into them.

Mrs. Sandell, the president, spoke first. "Lacey Lambert, your language and actions are inappropriate for this event."

"They are? And telling me I didn't deserve to be married to Randy and that it was all my fault that we divorced was appropriate?" Her pulse hammered through her veins and the hairs on the back of her neck rose. If they thought they could intimidate her, they had another think coming.

The women glanced over their shoulders and back at her. Mrs. Rutherford whispered. "We meant no harm."

"Really?" With a dozen retorts streaming through her head, Lacey clamped down hard on her tongue and held it for a long moment before saying, "You know when I came here this afternoon, I thought I had something to prove to you all. But now I realize, I only had something to prove to myself. I don't need you, or your club or your approval. You're just a bunch of lonely old women trying to fill your boring lives with the troubles of others. You pitied me once. But really I pity you more." When Mrs. Sandell opened her mouth to say something, Lacey lifted her hand. "Don't worry, I'm leaving."

Lacey refused to slink out the back the way she'd come in. Instead she walked slowly across to Audrey and Jackson. "Thank you for encouraging me to get that off my chest. Now, I'm leaving."

"Wait." Audrey grabbed her arm. "You have to stay a little longer. I hear they have a string quartet." She glanced over Lacey's shoulder. "Please stay a bit longer."

"I can't. I don't fit in here. These people don't care about me."

"I do." Audrey hugged her.

A motorcycle engine revved, breaking through the quiet chatter of the crowd. A moment later, a gleaming white Harley screamed into the garden and across the lawn, aiming for Lacey.

The driver wore jeans, a white shirt and a white cowboy hat, and a sexy wide grin as he spun around and came to a stop in front of her.

"Nick?"

"Not Nick. I'm your knight on a gallant white steed, here to rescue you. Hop on." He twisted the handle and the engine roared.

Her pulse thumped hard in her veins and a flock of butterflies swarmed her belly. Nick had come to rescue her? "But I'm wearing a dress."

"Good, you'll give them more to talk about than the back of that thing. Come on, baby, I have someplace special I want to show you and then we'll ride each other for the rest of the night." He lifted his cowboy hat and shouted. "Yahoo!"

"Why?"

"Because I want you in my life. I like you and could be well on my way to loving you." He scooted forward on the seat. "Now, are you getting on or am I going to ride away alone?"

"You like me?" Lacey swayed toward him.

"Did you catch the part about maybe being in love with you?" Audrey shoved her forward. "The man wants you. You want him. Go!"

Lacey lifted her skirt, remembering at the last second that she'd forgone panties to save her from an embarrassing panty-line beneath the skin-tight garment. As she slid onto the seat, her pussy creamed at the vibration of the engine beneath her. She wrapped her arms around Nick's waist and held on as he goosed the engine and spun out of the yard.

As they left the party behind, the sound of applause followed. Lacey glanced over her shoulder.

All the women, except maybe Mrs. Biedel, Mrs. Sandell and Mrs. Rutherford, were clapping and wiping tears from their eyes. They were clapping for her.

Joy rose up in Lacey's throat and she shouted to the sky, her head flung back, her breasts pressed firmly to Nick's back.

"You okay back there?"

"More than okay. I'm perfect."

"I'll second that." He drove onto the highway and turned off again after going only half a mile farther. He came to an open gate with a big arched entrance.

"Where are you taking me?"

"Look up."

The letters on the gate were large and it took her a moment to piece them together while sitting so close. "Second Chance Ranch?" She shook her head. "Who does it belong to?"

"Me." He clamped his cowboy hat down and took off before she could say another word.

When he pulled up in front of a large, limestone and cedar ranch house, Lacey could only stare, her mouth open. "This is yours?"

"Yes, ma'am." Nick set the kickstand in place and held Lacey's hand as she dismounted, then he slung his leg over the bike's seat and sat sideways on the bike. "Was the rescue a little too over the top?"

She smiled, happiness and confusion warring inside her. "It was great. But why?"

"I heard, from certain friends of yours, that it would take a knight on a white horse sweeping you off your feet to convince you to give love a second chance." He took off the white cowboy hat and waved a hand at the white Harley. "Do you know how hard it is to get your hands on a white Harley?"

She shook her head, tears welling in her eyes. "No." Her hands trembled and she was afraid her knees would give out. "Why did you do it?" she asked again.

Once again, Nick saved her from embarrassment by tugging her hand, forcing her to lean into him. "After my divorce, I didn't think I'd ever fall in love again, nor did I really want to." He tucked a strand of her hair behind her ear. "Then you showed up in my brother's apartment, bent on sex without strings." He chuckled. "I'd never met a woman like you. You're tough, you're tender, you speak your mind and you don't give a damn what people think about you."

"That doesn't sound like a good thing."

His arms tightened around her, his cock nudging her bottom. "And you're sexy as hell, and you make a great walking partner on a clear moonlit night. All of those attributes are what keeps me coming back for more." He eased her onto his lap. "I don't know what's going on between us, or where it will go. All I do know is that for every minute I'm away from you, I'm counting the minutes until I see you again. I like you, Lacey, and I think I might be well on my way to loving you, if you'll give me a chance."

She smiled and cupped his chin. "What happened to the fact you weren't looking for a relationship?"

"You happened." He kissed her, running his fingers through her hair to cup the back of her neck and bring her closer. When he let her breathe again, he asked, "So, are you game to give love a second chance?"

"Let me up." She pushed against his chest, stood and straightened her skirt, her lips pressed into a thin line.

NICK'S HEART PLUMMETED. He'd gone all out, finding the Harley when he really wanted a horse to ride on but unable to locate a white one at the last minute. After baring his soul to her, he couldn't think of anything else. Audrey and Cory were wrong. Lacey wasn't interested in strings. She'd said so herself.

He braced himself for her answer, praying he was wrong and that she was ready to try for love.

"Let me get this straight." She lifted one finger. "You're not down-and-out because of losing half your worldly goods to your ex in your divorce."

He shook his head. "No. I had to sell my last place to split the proceeds. I was staying with Cory until the construction crew finished my house. Didn't I tell you?"

She shook her head. "Must have slipped your mind." Lacey raised another finger. "You own an auto repair shop and it pays for all of this? Are you operating a chop shop on the side?"

He laughed. "No. After my divorce, I invested my half of the sale of our home in the stock market and promptly quadrupled my investment. I needed something to keep me busy while I looked for another ranch and built my house. I owned the shop and when the mechanic quit, I took over."

"I feel as if I don't even know who you are." Lacey rested her hands on her hips.

"You know how I feel about lying. You know that I like walking beneath the stars with a pretty girl and skinny-dipping in the moonlight. You know that I've always wanted my own horses and that I want to live on a ranch."

"True. Is there anything else you haven't told me I should know about?"

He captured her wrist and tugged her close. "That I care a lot about you and I wouldn't have driven into a garden party on a Harley for just anyone."

"Even Julia?"

"Especially not Julia." He laughed. "I still can't get over your walking into my apartment completely naked with my ex standing there, her mouth hanging open. I think that was the moment."

"What moment?" Lacey lifted the hem of her skirt and straddled his legs.

His cock strained against the confines of his jeans. He sucked in a breath and let it out slowly. "The moment I knew."

She leaned back, unhooked his belt buckle and slid his zipper down. "Knew what?"

Nick's cock sprang free. "That I couldn't lose you. That you were the gal for me." He lifted her up, wrapping her legs around his waist, his cock nudging her entrance. "So what do you say?"

Lacey rested her hands on his shoulders and leaned her forehead against his. "Have you ever done it on a Harley?"

He shook his head. "No. But I have a feeling I'm about to."

"Damn right." She lowered herself down over him, taking him in all the way to the hilt.

"Question is, are you game to give love a second chance?" he asked again.

"I don't know that I was ever really in love the first time. I think I was in love with the idea of love and marriage. So I can't say that I'm giving love a second chance."

Nick held still, afraid to get too far into her without some sort of pledge on her part. "Baby, you're killing me."

"Not yet, I'm not. We have a lot more to try before we die." She kissed him hard, her tongue snaking out to slide along his. When she broke off, she whispered in his ear, "Game on, cowboy, but no sloppy seconds. I'm in it for a first shot at real love."

"That's all I ask, sweetheart." He gripped her hips, and stood.

"I thought we were going to do it on a Harley."

He turned her around so that she was sitting on the bike. "You bet we are."

**If you enjoyed this book, try the other books in the
Ugly Stick Saloon Series**

Boots & Chaps (#1)
Boots & Sex Ed (#2)
Boots & Leather (#3)
Boots & Promises (#4)
Boots & Bareback (#5)
Boots & Dirty Tricks (#6)
Boots & Lace (#7)
Boots & Roses (#8)
Boots & Buckles (#9)
Boots & the Wishes (#10)
Boots & Twisters (#11)
Boots & the Bachelor (#12)
Boots & the Rogue (#13)
Boots & the Heartbreaker (#14)
Boots & Wings (#15)

BOOTS & ROSES

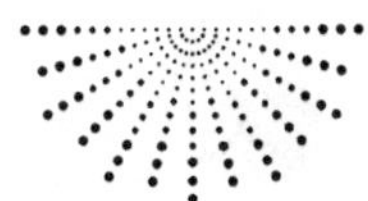

UGLY STICK SALOON SERIES BOOK #8

New York Times & *USA Today*
Bestselling Author

ELLE JAMES

writing as

MYLA JACKSON

BOOTS
&
ROSES
UGLY STICK SALOON
New York Times Bestselling Author
ELLE JAMES
writing as
MYLA JACKSON

CHAPTER ONE

"The Women's Aid Society should make a killing off this fundraiser." Bunny Leigh sat with her back to the bar, her gaze glued to the stage. Despite her best effort to remain detached, she couldn't help but get caught up in the insanity going on around her at the Annual Cowboy Auction.

"No kidding." Charli Sutton paused long enough at the bar to drop the dirty glasses and order the next round for the tables she waited. "You did a great job on the decorations."

Bunny shrugged. "It's the least the Sweet Temptations Flower Shop could do. Heck, Audrey offered up the Ugly Stick Saloon for the event, and giving away one free drink per customer was brilliant."

"Yeah, the drinks will grease the wheels for bidding. Her crowning glories were recruiting the cowboys..." Charli nodded toward the exit, "...and hiring the hottest deputy in the tri-county area to keep it sane."

Bunny glanced at Jack Monahan, the best-looking deputy on the sheriff's force, and her cheeks heated. He'd stopped by her flower shop on a regular basis to buy flowers for his mother. What a guy. Sensitive and handsome, with his dark hair and big brown eyes rimmed with lashes a girl would give her eyeteeth for. If Bunny was interested in dating, he'd be one of the local bachelors at the top of her list. Not that he'd be interested, and Bunny wasn't the type of girl to ask and risk rejection.

Two years since her divorce seemed too soon for Bunny to get used to the idea of dating again. Yet two years had been plenty of time for her ex to take the plunge. The bastard was getting married, already. Not that she cared about Ray anymore. Not since he'd cheated on her with the cute little dental hygienist he was now engaged to.

With a sigh, Bunny dragged her gaze from Jack and stared down at the program, running through the list of names. "Wow, she really struck gold. I don't think I've ever seen such a great lineup."

"Yeah." Charli smiled. "It's too bad I'm engaged, or I'd bid."

Bunny's brows rose, a smile curling her lips. "What, you don't think Connor would let you go out on a little ol' date with one of them?"

"Not no, but hell no." Charli frowned. "I may be taken, but there are a lot of single women in this room who aren't. And I know for a fact some of them have been savin' all year for this."

Bunny panned the room. Women of all shapes and

sizes crowded every bit of floor space in the saloon, each carrying a paddle with a number on it, ready for when the bidding started.

"Gotta get back to work. Everyone's already gone through their first-round freebie. They're into round two, and the fun hasn't even started." Charli grabbed a tray of beer mugs and hurried back out into the sea of raging estrogen.

Audrey Anderson, the owner of the Ugly Stick, leaned over the bar. "Can I get you another beer?"

Bunny stared at her mug, surprised to see it was empty. "Sure. But it'll have to be my last. I have to drive."

"No worries. The Gray Wolf brothers are lined up to provide free rides home to anyone who isn't fit to drive."

"Thanks." Bunny smiled. "We'll see how it goes." She'd never had so much to drink that she couldn't drive. She didn't plan on it now.

Audrey filled Bunny's mug from the tap and set it on the bar in front of her. "Where's your number?"

Bunny snorted. "Don't need one. I'm not bidding."

"What?" Audrey shook her head. "You've been divorced for two years now. It's about time you started dating again."

With another sigh, Bunny lifted her mug and sipped the golden brew before responding. "After the disaster of my marriage, why would I want to jump back into a relationship? I like where I am in life. I don't need a man to make me happy."

"Ray Zinke was a jerk. You did the right thing by divorcing him," Audrey said, as she wiped the bar with a clean rag. "Besides, not every man is a dirt bag like Ray. Look at Jackson. He's one hundred percent awesome. And his brothers Luke and Mark rank right up there with him."

Although Bunny had thought about the Gray Wolf twins and their swarthy, Native American good looks, she'd learned by experience that looks weren't everything. And unfortunately, Libby the bartender had the corner on the twin market. "They're taken."

"Maybe so, but they're good examples that not all men are cut of the same dumbass cloth. You have to give other men a chance."

Bunny shook her head. "No, I don't."

"What about companionship?"

"I can get a dog," Bunny was quick to quip, but there was the rub. A dog might be good company, but she missed having someone to talk to at night after work. Someone to hold her and whisper sweet nothings in her ear.

Audrey frowned. "What about partnership? Someone to share your life?"

"I almost lost half my business to Ray when he left me. I'm still paying him back a little at time and probably will be paying for the next decade. No partners."

With a soft harrumph Audrey shot back, "Okay... what about sex?"

"I own a nifty array of vibrators." Bunny lifted her chin, daring Audrey to challenge her lie. She only had one. "I can have sex any time I want. I'm responsible for my own orgasms, thank you very much."

Audrey frowned. "It's not the same."

"Audrey, I'm not looking for a man in my life right now." Bunny might not have been looking, but Audrey was hitting too close to home. The last couple of weeks, she'd been in the dumps going home to an empty apartment every night. No one to talk to. No one to share her day with.

"Well, if you change your mind, I took the liberty of signing you up for the auction." Audrey slapped a numbered paddle on the counter. "Think about it. It's just a date." She walked away, shaking her head.

Bunny sighed. Why couldn't people believe she was happy living alone?

Because you're not.

The thought came out of the blue and wedged in Bunny's craw, bringing her down when she should have been enjoying the anticipation of the auction's kickoff. She loved watching the bachelor cowboys roped into participating. The area had its fair share of handsome, single men, although they seemed to be getting younger every year.

Another sigh escaped Bunny's lips.

"Hey, pretty lady, what's gotcha down?" a warm, sexy voice said behind her.

She turned toward the bar and smiled at Cory McBride, her part-time flower deliveryman. "Just thinking."

"If you're thinking about me, I'd hope the frown would turn upside down." He winked and smiled, his full, sensuous lips curling ever so slightly.

Enough to make Bunny want to taste them.

Holy hell! I didn't just think that, did I?

"No, I was just trying to decide whether I would bid on a cowboy."

"Then save your money for me." He puffed out his chest, which was clad in a crisp white shirt that disappeared into neatly ironed blue jeans. The ridge beneath his fly stood out against the soft, dark denim. "I'm one of the cowboys being auctioned, along with a special surprise."

Bunny's heart flipped against her ribs and her belly tightened. She'd had a secret lust for this young man since he'd started working for her several months ago.

Her gaze slid over his broad shoulders and down to his narrow waist. Not that he was a boy. At twenty-one, he was more of a man than her ex-husband had ever been, and Cory was proud of his body, not at all shy about showing off the rippling muscles and taut abs.

And he had a lot of reasons to be proud of that glorious body.

Bunny dropped her gaze to her beer, afraid Cory would see his boss drooling if she didn't get a grip on her unfulfilled longing. "I'll leave the bidding to the younger girls. Can't have Temptation calling me a cougar now, can I?" She smiled up at him and immediately regretted it.

Cory's eyes narrowed. "What, you're all of twenty-six?"

"Not that it's any of your business." She ran her finger along the rim of her mug. "I'm twenty-seven." She held her breath, waiting for his gasp. It didn't come.

He shook his head. "You're not old."

"Older than you." She sighed. Damn she'd done a lot

of that this evening. What was wrong with her? "I've been married and divorced, and I own my own business. I feel like Methuselah."

"Hardly. For the record, there's only a little more than five years difference in our ages. And although I haven't been married and divorced, I've owned my own business since I was nineteen."

Bunny frowned. "Really?"

Cory's lips spread in a sensuous smile. "I'm a waiter and stripper here at the Ugly Stick, but I've been investing my money since I started working and have quite a personal portfolio. I'm financially independent. And, as you know, I just graduated with my degree in pre-med biology and I'm heading to medical school in Dallas next fall."

"Yeah, I know. I'll be losing my deliveryman." She sighed. Having Cory around had been fun, and the shop wouldn't be the same without his smiling face. "That's quite the resume. But that doesn't erase the fact I'm five years older than you."

"Look, sweetheart, between you and me..." He leaned across the bar, his face inches from hers. Cory's thick, golden mane flowed down around his shoulders, and blue eyes as clear as a summer day shined into hers. "I'd rather go out with you than any other woman in this place."

Suddenly unable to breathe, Bunny closed her gaping mouth and licked her lips. The scent of his after-shave swirled around her and made her want to tip forward and plant her lips on his.

He winked. "Don't sell yourself short, darlin'. You've

got a lot more to offer than a twenty-one-year-old." Cory leaned closer and kissed her startled lips, then straightened. "You are a beautiful, warm and generous woman. What's not to love?"

Her mouth tingled from where his lips had touched, and she clenched her fingers to keep from reaching across the counter and claiming a do-over on that brief kiss.

"Now, if you'll pardon me, I have to go get undressed for my turn on the stage." He tapped her numbered paddle. "Think about it."

How the hell could she think with her brain fried by one little brush of his lips?

Charli swung by, her eyes wide. "Did I see what I think I saw?"

Heat climbed up Bunny's neck and into her cheeks. "No. No, you didn't see anything."

"I did! Cory kissed you, didn't he?" Charli dropped her tray on the counter and gave her order to Libby, before turning to grab Bunny's hands. "He never comes on to women. They always come on to him."

"So?" Bunny pushed her hair behind her ear. "He delivers flowers for me. It was just a friendly peck, like a handshake."

"My rosy butt it was." Charli's face split into a wide grin. "What did he say to go with that kiss?"

"Nothing," Bunny lied. "It wasn't a kiss." She lifted her mug to her lips, hoping it would give Charli the hint that she didn't want to discuss Cory anymore.

"You have to bid on him," Charli insisted, hiking her tray of drinks onto her shoulder.

"I don't have to do any such thing."

The band struck up a tune.

Charli's head jerked up and she set her full tray back on the counter. "Ah, that's my cue. I'm the MC."

Bunny sucked in a deep breath and let it out. *Whew. Saved by the music.*

Audrey hurried forward. "I'll get your orders, Charli. Get on out there before the women riot."

"Goin'." Charli nodded toward Bunny as she passed. "Make sure she bids on Cory. He kissed her."

Audrey's brows rose. "Cory kissed you?"

Bunny wanted to trip Charli for her parting comment. Now she'd have to face the Audrey inquisition. She raised her hand. "Please. It was just a peck. We're only friends."

With a laugh, Audrey gathered the tray Libby had filled with beer mugs and glasses of wine. "Okay. I get it. Don't push you. Still, if not Cory, consider bidding on someone else. There are plenty of handsome cowboys who will be strutting their boots and buckles across the stage." Audrey took off, carrying the heavy tray as if it weighed nothing, her long strawberry blond hair swaying sassily.

Alone in a saloon full of women, Bunny watched as one cowboy after another stood on the stage, removed his shirt and played up the crowd. The shouts and screams grew louder as the liquor flowed and bidding became more intense.

Twice, Deputy Jack Monahan had to break up a fight between several of the women. He was starting to look a little harried since he'd had his ass pinched on more than one occasion.

Bunny found herself wishing she was close enough to pinch as well. As soon as the thought crossed her mind, she straightened. She'd drooled over two handsome men tonight. Like Audrey said, she probably needed to get out more often. Maybe it was time for her to start dating again. Hell, Ray was getting married in three days. He'd definitely moved on. Why not her?

After the first couple of men were auctioned, Jack made his way to the bar where Bunny sat.

"Can a guy get an ice cold…water?" He sighed. "Rather have a beer, but I'm afraid the ladies would take advantage of me."

Libby chuckled, handing Jack a mug of ice water. "Audrey needs to hire ugly cops for this party. You're too damned good looking to keep the peace."

The man is riot material, Bunny added silently. Her body flushed with heat at the deputy's nearness, and she struggled for something to say.

Jack leaned across Bunny and snagged the mug in his fist, his broad shoulders filling her vision. "Mind if I sit?" He eased onto the stool beside Bunny. "Gonna bid tonight?"

Sitting beside the handsome deputy, Bunny's heartbeat fluttered for the second time that night. "I hadn't planned on it."

Jack winked. "Be a shame. I know for a fact any one of those cowboys would be proud as punch to be bought and paid for by you." He set his mug down and tapped his chest. "Why, if I was gonna be up there, I'd hope and pray it was your paddle rising to stake a claim on me."

Bunny's gut knotted, and her body trembled at his softly spoken words. She reminded herself there were a lot of prettier women in the saloon, and her lips twisted. "I bet you've told half the women in this bar the same thing. Did Audrey put you up to advertising as well as busting up fights?"

He raised his hand Boy Scout style and shook his head. "No one put me up to it. You're the first woman I've said that to and the last." He leaned close until his lips almost brushed her ear. "You're the only florist I buy my roses from."

"Jack, I'm the only florist in town." Bunny crossed her arms. "You're in my shop at least once a week, supposedly buying flowers for your mother. How many girlfriends are you really buying for?"

A dark shadow flashed in his eyes, and his smile slipped for a second then was back in full force. "That's for me to know and you to find out." He winked, tossed back another long swallow of water and stood. "If you'll excuse me, I have a job to do." Jack lifted her hand and gazed into her eyes. "Just for the record, you're the prettiest woman in this joint."

Heat rose up Bunny's neck into her cheeks. "Liar."

His eyes narrowed. "Another one for the record…I never lie." He pressed his lips to her fingers and warmth spread throughout Bunny's body.

Out of the corner of her eyes, she could see the women on either side of her gaping, and more heat burned into her cheeks.

Jack lifted his head and brushed his lips across hers, then captured her bottom lip in between his teeth, sucking it into his warm, wet mouth. When he let go, he smiled. "That's just a sample."

Too stunned to form a coherent comeback, Bunny licked her lip in dumb silence, her gaze following Jack across the crowded floor until he was swallowed up in the surge of women.

Two men had flirted with her in one night. An anomaly for sure, but a great boost to her otherwise faltering ego. Maybe coming to the Ugly Stick Saloon had been a good idea after all. It was helping take her mind off the two-year anniversary of her divorce and her ex's pending nuptials.

Cory tightened his chaps in the dressing room behind the stage, his lips still tingling from the kiss he'd given Bunny. He'd wanted to run his hand through her long, silky brown hair and tug just enough to expose the beating pulse at the base of her throat. And that was just the beginning of all the things he wanted to do with her.

"Hey, no fair on kissin' my girl." Jack stood at the entrance to the backstage area, his arms crossed over his uniformed chest.

"Told you I was serious about making my move."

"Yeah, but did you have to kiss her?"

Cory grinned. "I wanted her to be certain of my intentions." He crammed a cowboy hat on his head and stood straight. "I only have a couple weeks before I head to Dallas for med school."

Jack shook his head. "Then why get involved now? I

thought you were gonna stay single until you were through all that."

Cory's lips tightened. "For the first time in my life, I know what I want."

Jack sighed. "Bunny?"

With a nod, Cory slipped a vest over his broad chest. "If I wait until I'm through med school, she could go off and marry someone else. I have to let her know how I feel now. If she's even slightly interested, maybe she'll wait."

"What about me?" Jack spread his hands wide. "You and I both know I don't buy flowers for my mother. She's allergic."

"Look, I know you like her." Cory stared at his friend. "If you want her and she wants you, I'll step back and leave it at that. You're the best friend I've ever had, and I'd want both of you to be happy. But if I have even a smidgeon of a chance with her, I'm going for it."

"How 'bout letting her choose?"

"That's kinda what I had in mind." Cory grinned. "You and I have shared a woman before. But this is different. I want something long term. I want to know she'll be there for me, to go the distance."

"And I don't?"

Cory shrugged. "You haven't had a steady relationship since before I knew you."

Jack tipped his head. "Just because I haven't had a steady woman, doesn't mean I don't want one."

"Are you tellin' me you're over what happened to Stacy?"

Jack's lips tightened and he glanced to the far corner.

"Sorry." Cory laid a hand on his arm. "I know it hurts to talk about her."

Stacy had been Jack's girlfriend in college. They'd been inseparable from the moment they'd met. She'd died in a senseless accident that almost cost Jack his own life. When he'd woken up a week later, he'd missed the funeral. He'd also missed any opportunity for closure or goodbyes.

Jack had dropped out of school and gone to work. Stripping. He'd been on a collision course with hell until he met Cory.

Jack shook off Cory's hand and stepped away. "I don't really think I'll ever be over her. But that doesn't mean I can't get on with my life."

Cory slung an arm over Jack's shoulder. "There's not much I won't share with you, man, but Bunny is special."

"Don't I know it." Jack glanced across at Cory. "Since Stacy died, Bunny's the first woman I can't forget about when I close my eyes at night. I'm one kick in the pants short of falling in love with her, if I haven't already."

Cory nodded. "Then we have a problem."

Jack frowned. "Yeah, both of us want her, but only one of us can have her—if the woman is amenable."

Cory stared straight ahead. "You and I have been pretty close, gone through a lot together and been there for each other, right?"

With a nod, Jack answered, "Yup."

"You taught me how to defend myself."

Jack rubbed the back of his neck. "And you kicked

my ass until I went back to school and finished my degree."

"We're so close we're joined at the hip in investments, and we're goin' in half on the same piece of property."

"Yeah. So?"

"What do you say we give Bunny the choice? If she's willing, she can have either one of us...or both."

His frown deepening, Jack seemed to chew on Cory's words before he responded. "I know we shared Maxy Palmer last year when we went to Fiesta in San Antonio. It was fun and all, but this is Bunny we're talkin' about, not a one-night stand."

"I know that." God, he knew that. "And I don't want to scare her off any more than you do."

"Then how's this gonna work?"

"I'm not exactly sure, but Mark and Luke Gray Wolf share Libby and she seems more than happy with the arrangement," Cory said. "I don't see why we can't share Bunny."

Jack's lips twisted. "From what I've seen of Bunny, she's not as free-spirited or streetwise as Libby. I don't think she'll go for it."

Cory let his arm drop from Jack's shoulders and turned to face his friend, the idea blossoming. "It only makes sense. We're both interested in her, right?"

Jack nodded. "Looks that way."

"We're as close as two men can get." Cory grinned. "Hell, you're family, like my brother Nick."

"Same to you, man." Jack's lips lifted in a half-cocked

smile. "So you think we can share Bunny and not jack up our friendship?"

"I can, if you can." Cory stuck out his hand. "But it's still up to Bunny."

Jack stared at Cory's hand, then gripped it in a firm handshake. "Deal." He pulled Cory into a bear hug.

Cory pulled back and clapped his hands together. "We got us a woman to court."

"How are we gonna do that?" Jack asked.

A slow smile slid across Cory's face. "It's all part of my plan."

Jack frowned. "I was afraid of that."

For forty-five minutes, Bunny left the paddle on the bar, refusing to give in to her loneliness and bid on a paid-for pity date. One by one the men paraded around the stage, women bid and the gavel banged. One by one the chance for a date passed and Bunny slipped deeper into a blue funk.

Her lips still tingled from the contact with Cory's and Jack's, and she raised her hand to touch her mouth. No vibrator had affected her as much as those earth-shaking kisses. Once again, Bunny considered Audrey's words. Maybe it was time for her to get out in the dating pool again and give love a second chance.

"Hold on to your belt buckles, ladies," Charli said with a flourish. "Here to introduce the final act, the woman who made the Cowboy Auction possible, Audrey Anderson."

Audrey stepped up on the stage with Deputy Monahan holding her arm. The owner of the Ugly Stick

Saloon took the microphone from Charli and faced the crowd, her face straight, serious. "Ladies, it's been brought to my attention that we've had several instances of sexual misconduct against our own Deputy Jack Monahan. I ask you to please keep your hands to yourself and respect the man who was brought here to keep the peace."

One woman yelled, "Boo!"

The room full of women joined her, all shouting, "Boo!"

Bunny smiled. If she wasn't mistaken, Audrey had something up her sleeve and she was playing the audience.

Audrey winked. "Oh, so you like playing dirty?"

As one, the women yelled, "Hell, yeah!"

"Then let's raise the stakes. For the first time in Cowboy Auction history, we're offering up a two-fer."

The ladies roared their approval.

Despite her resolve to remain unaffected by the goings on in the saloon, Bunny leaned forward, a tingle of anticipation rippling through her body. Cory hadn't been offered up for auction yet and he'd hinted at a surprise. Was this it?

"All our cowboys have been fabulous sports about this auction, but the last bidding opportunity we're offering tonight is special and near and dear to my heart. Please welcome the two-fer deal of Cory 'The stripper so hot you'll singe your fingers' McBride..."

Cory danced out on the stage, wearing a vest, boots and leather chaps over a black G-string. The only thing not showing was his package, and it was swelled enough to give every woman enough information to go on. The man was hung.

Bunny sucked in a breath and held it while her pulse pounded so loud she could barely hear herself think. Her deliveryman had been in her sex dreams and fantasies more and more often lately. Now this... Holy smokin' cowboys!

Audrey continued, "The other half of this dynamic duo is our very own man of peace, Deputy 'Pull over and let me frisk you' Jack Monahan!" Audrey handed the microphone back to Charli.

Deputy Monahan joined Cory center stage, slipping his uniform shirt off, exposing shoulders as broad as Cory's and equally tanned and gleaming with a fine layer of oil.

Holy rock stars! Between the Adonis blond beauty that was Cory and the dark, rugged sex appeal of Jack, Bunny could barely breathe.

The crowd exploded in a frenzy, all the paddles raising in the air as the bidding started.

Bunny perched on the edge of her stool, her body trembling.

The two men danced around the stage in sync to bump-and-grind music barely audible over the cacophony of women yelling and whistling.

Bidding started at five hundred dollars and shot up from there.

Not that I'm interested in bidding. Bunny mentally calculated what she had in her bank account.

Audrey handed the numbered paddle to Bunny. "I'll match you dollar for dollar." She shrugged. "I won't keep one of them, but I want to contribute to the cause. This way I can, and Jackson won't have heartburn about it."

"I can't bid on those two. I wouldn't know what to do with one man, much less two!"

Audrey's brows rose. "Seriously? Oh, honey, you really do need to get out more often. Did I ever tell you about the day I danced for Jackson, Mark and Luke on Jackson's thirtieth birthday?" She tugged at the front of her shirt. "And I don't mean two-stepping." Audrey fanned herself. "Making me hot just thinkin' about it."

"Audrey, you're much more free-spirited. I'm… I'm…" Bunny glanced down at the paddle in her hand. "Not."

A soft hand rested on Bunny's shoulder and Audrey leaned close. "How do you know if you've never tried to be?"

Bunny shrugged. "I've always focused on getting my business going, getting my finances straight—"

"Puttin' your lousy ex-husband through school. Yeah, I can see where that gotcha." Audrey shook her head. "That's all well and good when it comes to running a business, but what about givin' yourself a second chance at love?"

"I don't need a second chance. Once was bad enough. I don't think I'm ready to float that boat again." Although the two men on the stage could more than set her sails. Holy hell, they were built like brick houses, all muscle—hard, finely chiseled muscle.

"If not for love, then date for fun or a release from stress." Audrey threw her hand in the air. "Why not satisfy your sexual fantasies? Anything to get you out of your shell, girlfriend."

"One thousand dollars!" Charli shouted into the microphone. "Ladies, this is twice the spice for the money. Don't stop now." She nodded toward the throng. "One thousand one hundred from number forty-one."

"A thousand dollars?" Bunny did the math in her head. "I'd have to sell a lot of roses to afford those two."

"Raise your paddle. Remember, I'll double whatever you can afford."

Even as Bunny shook her head, her fingers tightened around the paddle's wooden stick. "I can't."

"Yes. You can. It's just a date," Audrey insisted. "Think about what Cory can do with that whip. And Jack has handcuffs."

Cory cracked the whip, and number thirty-seven raised her paddle, bumping the bid up another one hundred dollars.

Bunny's heartbeat accelerated. She had over two grand in savings for a rainy day and maybe to pay off her ex when she got a little more saved. That money was not earmarked for a hot date with two sexy men.

It still galled her to no end that Ray got half of her business in the divorce, Texas being a community property state. Out of the "goodness of his heart" Ray had let her keep the flower shop, as long as she paid him for his half over time, as a loan. He never let her forget it either, always giving her his unwanted opinion on how to run the flower shop. Spending so much money on a date would have him questioning her ability to stay in business. He might even foreclose on his loan.

"Going once," Charli said.

"What?" Bunny's breath caught and she leaned so far forward on her stool she almost slid off.

"Going twice." Charli paused. "They're a steal at twelve hundred dollars. Come on ladies, won't one of you bid thirteen hundred?"

Bunny's hand shook, her grip clenching on the paddle. Before she could analyze her actions, she raised her paddle.

"Is that Bunny Leigh back there near the bar?" Charli shielded her eyes from the glare of the stage lights. "Y'all gonna let Temptation's best florist go home with the two most drool-worthy men in the county?"

Cory and Jack stared across the room, straight at Bunny, both smiling.

Her pulse accelerated until she thought for certain her heart would jump right out of her chest. Her gaze panned the room, praying someone else would raise a paddle quickly before she bought the cowboy and the cop.

Charli grinned, and before anyone else could get a paddle above shoulder-high, she pounded her gavel on the podium and shouted, "Sold!"

ABOUT THE AUTHOR

Twenty years of livin' and lovin' on a South Texas ranch raising horses, cattle, goats, ostriches and emus left an indelible impression on Myla Jackson, one she likes to instill in her red-hot stories. Myla pens wildly sexy, fun adventures of all genres including historical westerns, medieval tales, romantic suspense, contemporary romance and paranormal beasties of all shapes and sexy sizes. She lives in the tree-covered hills of Northwest Arkansas with her husband of more than 20 years and her muses—the human-wanna-be canines—Chewy and Sweetpea.

To learn more about Myla Jackson and her alter ego Elle James visit:

www.mylajackson.com

mylajackson@mylajackson.com